DECKER HALLS

A DECKER CONNECTION CHRISTMAS NOVELLA

CHERYL CAMPBELL

Developmental Editing by Kara Merideth (Kat's Literary Services)

Copy and Line Editing by Kat Wyeth (Kat's Literary Services)

Proofreading by Paige Munnik (Kat's Literary Services)

Paperback ISBN: 979-8-9929865-4-9

Just because there's snow on the roof doesn't mean there's not a fire in the furnace.

After all, who do you think taught the Decker guys how to treat a woman?

CHAPTER ONE

SULLY

———

Ashleigh throws her head back, and her laughter carries across the room as she dances with her new husband and their friends. The smile on her face is unfettered joy, and it's everything I've ever wanted for my daughter. She's a vision in her white gown, her blonde tresses framing her face, her blue eyes sparkling with happiness. I can't hide my smile at this moment. My princess is married.

She spins around in circles, hand in hand with Cole, her new husband, as the full skirt of her dress swirls around the dance floor. My chest tightens as I remember her as a child, begging me to spin her around and around. She'd have the same look on her face. The memories are almost too much to bear. I take a deep breath and wipe the errant tear away.

During the ceremony, I tried to hold back the tears, but the feelings were overpowering. I locked down my emotions for years, and now that they're out, I don't think I can restrain them.

They threaten to start again, and I take another deep breath in an attempt to suck them back down.

Devlin Millbanks, my best friend and business rival, sits next to me and hands me a tissue. "She looks just like Rebecca."

"I know, Mills," I whisper. "A girl should have her mother, especially at her wedding. I wish she were here." So damn much. I'd give anything, everything, to have my wife back.

"She is," he says. "She's in Ashleigh's laugh, she's in Julian's charisma, and she's in Alexander's fierce loyalty. She's living through your kids, Sully. She's here. Right there. On the dance floor. Don't you see her?"

I nod slightly and wipe a hot tear from my eye. "I do."

And that's the problem. My heart aches thinking about how much Rebecca would have enjoyed today. Knowing I wasn't the best dad after she died makes the pain sharper. The guilt heavier. Of course she's with us. She always is.

After Rebecca died, I would see her everywhere. I'd hear a laugh and scour the restaurant to find her, only to scare a random woman. At ball games, I'd reach for her and find an empty chair beside me. So in order to cope with the devastating loss of my one true love, I shut down. Protecting myself from the pain, I locked down my emotions. It's easier not to feel the heartache every day when you're going through life numb.

I try not to think about what I've missed with the kids, but watching them together, my pride swells. They're all amazing, despite my absence. Sure, I was at important events like graduations and holidays. But I feel like I missed out on truly experiencing them. Today, I'm here for it all.

My daughter's wedding has rekindled my zest for life. Although, admittedly, it took too long. Regardless, I'm thankful it's happened. But man, my emotions are enjoying their newfound freedom and refuse to be locked up again. I'm on an emotional roller coaster, and it's a bit overwhelming.

"It's nice to see you smile again, Sully. It's been a long time." Mills is right. Although Rebecca died fourteen years ago of ovarian cancer, she left pieces of herself in our children. And she's never shone so brightly as she is today. That's why I'm such a mess. Hot mess express, right here. My usual stoicism has taken a vacation today.

"I thought you'd be busting my balls about crying like a baby." I can always count on Mills to keep it real with me.

"Nah, you've always been a crier. My god, you cried buckets at your own wedding. I wasn't sure you'd get through the vows," he says with a chuckle, lightening the mood. Mills and I have been friends since junior high, and he was my best man all those years ago. He watched my kids grow up and is the godfather and mentor to my middle child, Julian.

"I guess Cole and I have that in common. He'll fit in with this family just fine. Maybe I need to make him a Reaper after all?" Cole Davidson, Ashleigh's husband, is a songwriter and baseball player for the New York Liberties organization. Mills owns the Liberties, which are the rival baseball team to my Carolina Reapers.

Yep. Two best friends own rival baseball teams. You couldn't script a better friends-to-rivals story. When I made my first billion, I petitioned the MLB to put a team in Charlotte, and thirty years later, we have two World Series titles and were division champions this year.

When Ashleigh met Cole, she wanted to prove herself to the world beyond her family connections. I wanted Cole to have that independence, too, so Mills grabbed him up for his franchise instead of me making him a Reaper. Honestly, it was best for all parties involved.

"All you Decker men were a blubbering mess. Even Alexander. I'll admit, you guys had me choked up too."

I take a sip of my bourbon and watch my kids, a flood of emotions hitting me again.

"Alexander's been a blubbering mess since Dani and Tyler came into his life. I'm worried about him when she goes into labor because it will be out of his control. He treats her like she's made of glass."

Mills nods in agreement. "Dani told me she's having a girl, and that has sent him into a total girl-dad spiral." We laugh at the thought of my broody, grumpy son with a little girl. She'll have him wrapped around her tiny finger when she takes her first breath. And then, god help us all. Understandable. My princess did that to me too. My throat thickens, and I choke on the sense of regret that I let her down.

"Yeah, but he had good practice with Ashleigh since I wasn't as engaged as I should have been when she was younger." When Rebecca died, I died too. I withdrew and did the bare minimum for years. I'm not proud of it, but losing your soulmate is a pain I wouldn't wish on anyone. Fortunately, Alexander and Julian stepped up for Ashleigh. Now guilt has entered my emotional intervention session and is sitting next to grief and loneliness while giving the middle finger to regret and melancholy. It's a hell of an emotional party I'm having today.

"Enough of all that," Mills says sharply. "This is a new chapter in the life of Sullivan Decker. Your kids are all happy and living their best lives. When are you going to get back into the game and live yours?"

Mills has walked beside me as I've grieved, but for the past year or so, he's been encouraging me to find a life outside of work. He wants me to date again. How do you even do that at my age? I haven't been on a date since I met Rebecca in my senior year in college. That was another lifetime and thirty-eight years ago. I'm not the man I was then. I was invincible with Rebecca by my side. Her love was the catalyst for everything I did. I did it for her. For my family.

"I hear ya, Mills. I do. I'm headed up to the mountains for the holidays, and maybe I'll ask Santa for some dating advice this year. Hell, maybe he'll leave someone under my tree who's willing to put up with my sorry ass." I actually smile at my little joke. It's a whisper of a past me, a man who used to laugh. Mills looks at me thoughtfully, like he sees a ghost of his old friend.

"I don't know. I saw you dancing out there with Ash, and your ass didn't look too bad from where I was sitting."

"I'm flattered, but you're not my type, Mills."

We both laugh. The weight I usually have sitting on my chest lessens, and I'm breathing differently—fuller. And it must be obvious because Mills looks away from the spectacle on the dance floor to focus on me.

"So, you're going to be alone for the holidays?" Devlin doesn't try to hide his concern.

"Yeah, I've encouraged the kids to start their own traditions. It's Alexander's first Christmas with Tyler and Dani. Ashleigh and Cole will be on the West Coast for the next few weeks while he works on a record deal. And Julian's looking pretty content with Harper. I'll be fine. We've had some amazing family time this week." Pride was the first emotion to break out of my locked heart. Each of my kids is an amazing human being, blazing a trail through this world. They are loving and kind, just like my Rebecca.

"Well, you're welcome to come to New York and spend time with me and Brittney. You haven't really gotten to know her." Brittney is Mills's fourth wife and twenty years his junior. I think she's after a slice of his money, but as long as he's happy, that's all I care about. By this time, I assume he's got the prenup locked down. I can't ignore the irony that he wants to give me love and dating advice, but then again, he has found happiness in each of his marriages, at least for a few years.

"Appreciate it, but I'm going to do a few things around the house and…"

"Like what? You're about as handy as a glass hammer." He gives me his *I dare you to challenge me* CEO stare.

"Can you just be supportive, please?" I teasingly snap back. "I'm working on this new chapter and all. Who the fuck knows, maybe I'm meant to be a lumberjack or something." I'm a little old for a midlife crisis, but it's never too late to start over. This week convinced me I'm ready to bring my heart back to life, even if it's just to laugh with my friends and enjoy time with my grandchildren. Maybe it's time to let people back in and not be so damn lonely. Because, if I'm being honest, being emotionless isn't any way to go through life. Sure, it kills the pain, but it also kills the happiness, the joy, the love of days like today. I'm experiencing all the powerful emotions today, and I'm okay. Feeling is *living*.

Mills doubles over laughing, slapping his knee at the humor in my declaration. Okay, so maybe it's bold and delusional, but I'm not incompetent. I had my own tech start-up after college, currently chair two corporate boards, and own a Major League Baseball team. I'm a self-made man, and he knows it. Hell, we both are.

"What's got you laughing so hard, Uncle Mills?" Ashleigh asks. "I have to hear it." Her laughter blends with Mills's guffaw, and I can't help but laugh too. I'm sure she's more than curious. She probably thinks I'm losing it, since her typically distant father doesn't laugh much. Granted, it's the first time I've done that in a long time. It feels foreign, forbidden, and maybe a little rebellious. As I look at my beautiful daughter through my tears, I see my wife smiling at me. *Okay, Becks, I hear you. I'll always love you, but maybe it's time to let love back in my life again.*

CHAPTER
TWO

CYNTHIA

———

Millions of Americans are gathering around the table giving thanks or watching football in a food coma right now, but I'm alone, driving a rental car on a winding two-lane road in the North Carolina mountains, praying I find my destination before daylight slips away. Gripping the steering wheel until my knuckles are white, I concentrate on my GPS instructions.

"Turn right in five hundred feet," the disembodied voice orders.

"Where?" If there is any question that I'm losing it, I'm afraid I answered that by talking back to the GPS. I slow the car to prepare for my questionable turn. On my right, I see nothing but a wall of solid rock. The other side of the road has a dented guardrail of suspicious integrity. It gives drivers a false sense of security that it will save them from plunging to their deaths off the side of this mountain. How can there be a road or driveway in the next five hundred feet? I take one more hairpin turn and almost miss the wide opening on my right. Just like the GPS said. I should know better than to question technology.

I turn in, barely getting my car off the road, and come to an imposing gate blocking the road up the mountain. The driveway seems to go straight into the dark forest. I look at my text message from Grace, enter the code, and the gate slides open, allowing me to move forward.

When I told my best friend I needed to leave civilization for a while, she assured me this was the place. Apparently, I should be careful what I ask for when I'm around Grace. She took me literally. The last small town I drove through was at least ten miles down the mountain. This place is definitely off-the-grid.

I'm glad I listened to her when she insisted I get a four-wheel-drive rental from the Charlotte airport because this driveway wasn't made for regular cars. It's steep and windy, just like the road I turned off. It's so dark, my automatic lights come on even though it's only early afternoon. I'm questioning my sanity as I make my way further into the forest, the crunch of the gravel under my tires announcing my arrival to the woodland creatures. When Grace said I could stay at her brother's mountain house for a while, I should have asked for more details. She told me it was rustic but comfortable, and I assured her that's all I needed. Now, as I drive through the woods, I'm nervous to know if this place has indoor plumbing.

The phone rings in the car, the sound making me jump and hit the gas a little too hard, my tires throwing gravel into the woods.

"Grace, you scared the hell out of me," I say as a greeting, my tone sharper than I mean.

"Sorry, Cyn, I was just checking on you. Sounds like you're still driving?" Her concern fills the car.

"Yeah, I'm almost there." I debate asking about the plumbing when she continues on.

"Listen, I know it's not like your New York apartment or house in the Hamptons, but you'll be fine. Granted, you can't get delivery on a whim, but I've had the caretaker stock the house with groceries and your favorite snacks, and Devlin's wine cellar is at your disposal. And if you need help or anything, I mean anything, the caretaker lives in the small house on your way up."

As if she speaks it into existence, a house comes into view on my left. Um, it's not exactly the rustic log cabin I had pictured. It's a gorgeous chalet with an inviting front porch that faces the woods. The three-car garage isn't even disproportionate to the house. There's an SUV and an ATV parked in front. Smoke drifts lazily from the chimney. It's incredible. Peaceful.

Maybe I missed the small house, and this is the house I'm supposed to be at?

"I just passed a house, but now I'm thinking it's where I'm supposed to go?"

"No, silly, that's the caretaker's house. When you go around the corner, you'll see Dev's house. His is the one on the left, closest to the caretaker's house. You have all the codes, and if you need anything, I mean anything, just ask the caretaker. He's a little rough around the edges, but adorable. A little quiet, probably from living by himself most of the year, but very kind. And very handy. He can fix anything."

"There's another house up here?" I can't believe that because it feels so remote.

"Yes, but don't worry, it's probably empty." Before she can finish her sentence, the road opens into a clearing and splits to the right and left, leading to each house, if you can even call them that. The glass sparkles in the afternoon sun, each one an architectural marvel. They look more like resorts than individual homes. I feel silly even wondering about indoor plumbing now.

"Grace, this place is…" I stop my car in front of the enormous house that looks like a stone castle straight from the pages of a fairy tale. The double doors must be fifteen feet tall, and there's an actual turret with stained glass windows.

"Incredible, right? Devlin usually hides out there when he's between wives, which made me think it was perfect for you. I know Trey's wedding hit you harder than you're admitting, and it's understandable. Twenty-six years of marriage is a lot of your life. But friend, you'll be fine. Hell, better than fine. Fuck him and his teenage bride! Let her suck his wrinkly balls and decide if it's worth his money. Spoiler alert: it's not."

I laugh at Grace, almost to the point of snorting. She's exactly what a best friend should be—supportive and willing to bash my ex and say things I want to say but won't.

"You know I don't care about her. Or him."

And I really don't care. My marriage was over years ago. But as Grace reminds me, just because I gave him twenty-six years of my life, I still have some good years left in me. Unfortunately, as a fifty-four-year-old woman, it's difficult to start over. Men my age want women much younger. Case in point, my ex-husband.

It's my fault, really. I became comfortable with the dysfunction, which is sad to admit. But I married Trey, for better or worse. Granted, I didn't think worse meant a workaholic who would have multiple affairs. The more successful at work, the more money he made, the more entitled and horrible he became. But it was my reality, my choice to stay. The first time he had an affair, I confided in my mother. I was looking for direction, empathy—something. Her response? I should have picked a better husband. My choice. My consequences. So I stuck it out. Pretended like I didn't care until, finally, I didn't.

Our marriage became one of roles and duties. He was the high-powered divorce attorney representing the lying and cheating rich husbands of Manhattan, doing everything he could to leave the wives high and dry. Publicly, I was his dutiful wife, who kept his social calendar full of club functions and society gatherings. To the outside world, he was a doting husband, but to me, he was a roommate at best, a philandering womanizer at worst.

When Trey's latest fling got pregnant, he decided it was time to divorce me, marry her, and start a new family. He will have grandchildren older than his own child, but I guess that's a modern family these days.

Truth be told, I'm nervous but grateful as I start this new adventure. It's been a long journey of conforming to expectations, and I lost myself along the way. Now I've got the time for soul-searching and discovery. It's no longer a luxury but a necessity for me to move forward.

The fairy-tale castle's incredible grandeur fills me with wonder as I step inside, curious about how my story will unfold. Because that's the thing about fairy tales. The princess isn't looking to be rescued. She's on her own journey. Granted, most princesses aren't the stepmother who gave up her law career to raise the children of the wicked widower. But then again, I wouldn't expect my story to be traditional. And I highly doubt I'll find my Prince Charming here.

Yeah, maybe it's time to forget the fairy tale, dust off my law degree, and work on important things. Things that make a difference in the world. I'll get on that as soon as I figure out who Cynthia Newsome is supposed to be now that she's on her own.

CHAPTER
THREE

SULLY

———

I'm talking on the phone to Dave, our caretaker, and am surprised when I hear a car coming up the driveway. Since it's a private, gated road, no one comes here by accident. An SUV with Florida plates slows in front of the house and continues up the drive. The car veers to the left, and I assume it must be going to Mills's house.

"Sorry, Dave, what were you saying?"

"The electrician said the generator will keep your house warm enough to keep the pipes from freezing, but it doesn't have enough juice to be comfortable. Says it will be a few weeks before they can get the parts in to fix the electrical system. I'm sorry."

I was here for one night when the estate's electrical system died. Apparently, woodland creatures set up house in the main control panel, chewed through wires, and destroyed the computer chips that run the entire "smart house." Serves me right for putting high-end technology in a remote location.

I should have stuck to the basics and built a log cabin. It worked for the early settlers. Now, I'm no better off with all these modern conveniences. Decker Hall is basically a primitive cabin, thanks to a few chipmunks. Except the indoor plumbing still works. At least for now.

"It's fine. Honestly, it's probably for the best that I'm not rattling around in that big house by myself. Thanks for letting me stay at your place."

Dave's visiting family in Virginia for the next month, and since I don't have electricity, I'm staying at his house, at least until the electricity is fixed at mine. His mother's been sick, so I encouraged him to stay longer and spend time with her. Value the time you have with loved ones, I told him. That was first-hand experience talking.

"Ah, it's technically your place, Mr. Decker, but what's mine is yours. Literally. If you need me to come back and oversee the work, or do anything, I can."

Part of Dave's compensation for being the caretaker of Slugger's Summit is free housing on the property. It's a comfortable one-bedroom cottage with a full kitchen, a two-story living area that offers breathtaking views of the mountains, and a gigantic fireplace that provides both warmth and ambiance. Since he lives here year-round, the house is better stocked for the winter anyway. He has a large stack of firewood, split and ready to burn. It was much more practical than moving into Mills's house.

"No, no, you'll do no such thing. Spend the holidays with your family. I insist. I've got this. How hard can it be?" Dave gives a belly laugh that makes me question what I said to garner that reaction.

"I'll send you contacts for anything that may come up. Plumbing, electrical. Trees down. That kind of thing. Call any of my guys, and they'll be there to help in a jiffy. There's an app on my laptop to order groceries, and they usually deliver within a day or so. The housekeeper comes monthly during the winter, but she's off in December. So you may have to do your own laundry." I can hear the wince in his voice.

My first instinct is to bring my housekeeper from Charlotte up here, but I gave her the month off. Besides, there's nowhere for her to sleep.

I was in a very *Ebeneezer Scrooge on Christmas morning* kind of mood when I let everyone have the month off to spend with their families. I mean, it was the right thing to do, but now I'm in nature, fending for myself. Hell, I'm a fifty-eight-year-old man who runs major corporations. I'm not inept. I can do this. How hard can it be? Apparently hard enough to make a grown man laugh.

"Thanks, Dave. I'll be fine. But, hey, a car just drove past the house. Mills didn't mention coming up here. Is he having work done too?"

We bought this decades ago and named it Slugger's Summit. Our houses were built side by side, but each is as different as we are. His is more low-tech, mine is high-tech. Mine is a Norwegian-inspired smart home, with light woods, lots of glass, modern lines, and open spaces. To cater to my kids and their friends, I built an indoor/outdoor pickleball court, a pool, a rec room full of games, and amassed a DVD selection that would rival Blockbuster's—since it was built before the streaming era. The house features full automation. Well, it did until Alvin, Simon, and Theodore took it all down.

Mills's house looks like a medieval stone castle, complete with turrets and a dungeon. His home has the finer things in life, like a sauna, a gourmet kitchen, and a million-dollar wine cellar. And now, apparently, a mystery guest.

"No, sorry, I should have told you there's a guest staying there for a while. I had the house stocked before I left, so she should be fine."

"She? She's by herself?"

"As far as I know. If she needs anything, have her call me, and I'll handle it from here."

"Yeah, sure. I doubt I'll even see her. Hey, enjoy your family time. I'll be fine, too, you know."

"I'm not worried," he says with a chuckle as he hangs up.

A few minutes later, every hair stands on end as a blood-curdling scream fills the air.

I run outside and jump on the four-wheeler, taking it through the woods toward Devlin's house. My heart is racing as I rush up the hill.

When I come to a stop, I'm confronted with chaos on the front steps. Frantically swinging her arms, a woman performs a *there's a bug* dance as three tiny raccoons triumphantly scurry from her bag and into the woods. They join a larger raccoon who's waiting at the tree line to celebrate their stolen bounty. It looks like they got a pair of glasses, a pen, and a tube of something.

I suppress my newfound ability to laugh and clear my throat. "Everything all right here?"

As she turns, the soft afternoon light bathes her face, and I stop dead in my tracks, completely awestruck by what I see. I stare at her auburn hair, a wild mess, wondering if it's a delib-erate style choice or the result of the raccoon encounter. The soft texture of her hair is visible even from a distance. Her green eyes are glimmering, but I'm not sure if it's because of unshed tears or if they're always the color of shiny emeralds. But even amid the calamity, she's stunning.

She does that thing where she tugs on her jacket, rolls her shoulders back, and puts on airs of being prim, proper, and put together. It doesn't change a thing. She's still a gorgeous hot mess. She lifts her chin and acts like everything is fine, normal even, despite the scene of destruction before me.

"I left my bag for a few minutes while I unloaded the car and then, when I came back for it, they attacked." She says it calmly, as if she's giving a witness testimony and wasn't a participant in said attack.

A muscle in my jaw clenches as I bite my cheek, fighting back the smile threatening to break free. I take a few slow steps toward her, trying not to spook her. She looks like she's had a day. "Attacked?"

"Yes, attacked. One flew out of the bag and went for my sunglasses." She touches the top of her head, where her glasses must have been. "The others tried to take my bag, but I stopped them." I glance at the ground and find other victims of the attack, such as her glasses case, keys, and wallet.

"Well, I'm not sure the bag was quite their color." She looks down at the bag in question, studies it for a moment, giving the comment fair consideration, and gives a panicked laugh.

"No, I suppose it isn't. Honestly, it's not even my color, but it's a Birkin, so what can I do?"

I nod my head in solidarity because apparently, a Birkin explains everything. I smile at this woman who came screaming into my life. Literally.

I extend my hand for a handshake and introduction, but she holds the bag out to me instead. "Will you check for more creatures? I don't think I can take any more excitement today."

Looking in a woman's handbag is like breaching her inner sanctum. It feels intimate, personal. I hesitate. "Um, are you sure?"

"Very." I take the offensive item and hold it out between the two of us.

"Out of curiosity, what is your favorite color for a, um, Birkin, is it?" I want to distract her as I look into her bag. Inside, I find pieces of her life, shredded and ruined by the offending woodland creatures. Her makeup is open and smeared along the lining. Everything's covered in a sweet-smelling lotion, and the papers are all torn to shreds.

"I've always loved the vert jade, but you don't get to pick. Oh, but it doesn't matter." There's a stark contrast between her relaxed manner of speaking and the calamity unfolding around her. I'm fascinated by her ability to pretend this doesn't bother her because it obviously does. It's a behavior I know all too well.

Sighing deeply, she drops the act, her face softening into acceptance.

"I'll never be able to afford a new one again anyway." She releases a huge sigh. "And it's a ridiculously expensive extravagance when there are children who need help, and I guess I should sell it anyway, but now that nature has violated it, I've probably devalued it, and it's just another stupid thing I've done in the past forty-eight hours, and I'm sure the list will keep growing," she rambles.

Her unshed tears hang in the balance, and I'm paralyzed, unsure whether to fulfill my masculine duty and check her bag, hug her, or do anything to prevent her from crying. I'm afraid that if she loses control, I will, too, as my own feelings are fragile and unrestrained, much like an over-sugared toddler. They broke free at the wedding last week, and I haven't been able to bottle them back up. The one night I spent in my house, surrounded by pictures and memories, had me laughing and crying at the same time. Honestly, moving out of there was the best thing I could do for my sanity. I may permanently swap houses with Dave.

"I'll get you a new one, anything, but please don't cry," I blurt. I put my hands out, and the bag drops between us.

"That's sweet, but you, well, never mind," she starts. Her smile is warm, compassionate, kind. But the good news is that she's not crying. That's a win for me.

Reaching down, I grab the bag and toss it onto the ATV. I'll get it repaired, replaced, whatever it takes to keep a smile on her face. "I'm sorry you're having a hard time. Come on, let's get you inside, and I'll make you some hot chocolate. That'll make everything better."

CHAPTER
FOUR

CYNTHIA

———

I force myself to pull it together. I'm scaring this poor maintenance man, and it's just not fair to pull him into my drama. Although, to be honest, he looks more amused than scared. And he's not quite what I pictured when Grace described the caretaker. I pictured rugged, bearded, maybe a little unkempt, and younger. But this man. He's like boardroom meets flannel; his freshly shaven face highlights a chiseled jaw that suggests both power and ruggedness. His blue eyes sparkle with mischief as he peeks inside my bag. The fine lines around his eyes crinkle when he smiles. Graying at the temples, his dark-blond hair adds to his distinguished look. Yeah, he's not the mountain man I pictured, but he's more my type, if I have a type.

Now he's offered to make me hot chocolate. Which is an incredibly kind gesture, and it sounds fantastic, but I just met him. Is he safe? I can't believe I handed him my bag with my mace, and he tossed it onto his vehicle. Grace told me to call him for anything, and obviously, Devlin trusts him, so he must be safe, right?

"I'm so sorry. I must look a mess." My hair remains big and disheveled, despite my attempt to smooth it. Flashbacks to middle-school hair make me shudder.

"You've had a bit of an adventure." He gives me a once-over, a thorough look, but his kind eyes soften the scrutiny. Not judgmental at all. "Why don't you go get cleaned up, and I'll make that hot chocolate. Or would you prefer tea?"

"I don't even know if I have hot chocolate makings here." I take a deep breath.

"You do," he says confidently. "It's a winter staple here at Slugger's Summit."

I remember Grace telling me he stocked the kitchen. He knows more about this house than I do. When I arrived, I quickly scanned the bedrooms in a few short minutes, noting the size, layout, and light in each room before making my choice. I loved every single one, but for practicality, I chose the room closest to the stairs.

"Slugger's Summit, huh?" With Devlin's love of baseball, I get it. "Well, I appreciate the friendly gesture. That would be nice, thank you." His smile fills his face, and his eyes crinkle again. Whoa. I'm having a fantasy moment here.

"My pleasure." He holds out his hand. "I'm Sully, and I guess we'll be neighbors."

"Oh my gosh, where are my manners? Those creatures must have stolen them too." I reach out and take his hand. It's warm and smooth. I expected rough, calloused hands, but he doesn't seem to have the typical wear and tear of someone who does heavy lifting. He's a caretaker, not a lumberjack, I remind myself. He orders groceries. I scold myself for putting my preconceptions on him.

"I'm Cynthia Newsome. It's very nice to meet you. I'm not usually, well, this." I run my hand down my body to display my disastrous look.

"It's nice to meet you, Cynthia. And you look great. It takes a bit to settle in, and I'm sure it's different from Florida."

"Florida?"

"Sorry, I assumed, since the car has Florida tags?"

I can't help but laugh at his conclusion. "Rental from the Charlotte airport. I'm a New York City girl through and through."

"Well then, this place is certainly a culture shock. Come on, let's get you warmed up."

Sully heads to the kitchen, obviously familiar with the house. The scale of the rooms is so enormous that I'll definitely need my GPS to find my way around.

Returning to my bedroom, I hurl a suitcase onto the bed, the thud echoing in the quiet room, and rummage through it to find fresh clothes and toiletries. I gasp at my reflection. Pulling a twig from my hair only highlights how disheveled I am. A wave of nausea washes over me, my cheeks burning with a deep blush as I cringe at my appearance.

I'm not a vain person. But Trey had expectations, and over the years, I became conditioned to look a certain way. I wanted him to be proud to have me on his arm. Now, I want to look good for myself, to reclaim some semblance of self-confidence in this youth-worshipping world. Whoever said fifty is the new thirty is delusional. One more year, and I'll officially be in my mid-fifties. Gah!

A quick brush of my hair, a change of clothes, and a face wash, and I'm almost like new. I opted for an oversized cardigan and leggings, choosing comfort over fashion. New me. New look. With a shrug and a sigh, I turn away from the mirror.

When I finally get back to the kitchen, Sully is waiting with two steaming mugs of hot chocolate, the aroma rich and choco-latey, and a plate of chocolate chip cookies.

"Feel better?" he asks. His eyes scan me, and a smile of appreciation appears on his lips. I've seen that look before from Trey's colleagues and golf buddies. I must have cleaned up okay.

He slides a mug across the counter to me.

"Much. This smells terrific." A sip from my mug reveals a decadent richness, a wave of flavor that coats my mouth and awakens my taste buds. I can't stop myself as I let out a little moan of appreciation.

Immediately, the self-talk about watching calories creeps in, but I catch myself. No more. Not that I'm going to let myself go, but I'm so used to hearing Trey's comments and doing everything I could to avoid them. His manipulation ran deep.

What did you eat today? You look bloated. Women retain water, especially during their period.

Did you miss your hair appointment? It's looking dull. Age does that, but I'll get to the salon tomorrow.

That's not a very flattering nail color. It made me happy, but not anymore.

Have you thought about getting Botoxed? You're showing your age. I'm fifty-four. I can't compare to your latest secretary, but I've been trying.

After years of these comments, they've become the soundtrack of my life. But I'm not living that life anymore. It's time to rewrite the script and evict those thoughts. Starting with this hot chocolate.

"It's a special blend. You won't find it anywhere else." He says it like it's a secret, and I think he winked at me. Did he wink at me?

"Well, thank you for the hospitality. I promise not to be a bother."

"It's my pleasure. It can get a little lonely up here, so I welcome the company. How long are you staying?"

"I'm not sure. Until the new year, maybe?" The thing about running away is the lack of plans. No rules. Fresh start. For the first time, I have a fleeting thought that I may not want to go back.

"Hiding from the world or eluding the authorities? I won't

tell, either way." He raises his eyebrow, and I'm positive he winked this time. I can't stop the smile that breaks free.

"Not exactly hiding out, more like licking my wounds. Maybe a fresh start?"

He gives a brief nod, like he understands. Maybe that's why he chose this isolated retreat. "How do you know Devlin Millbanks?"

"I don't, not really. I mean, I've met him socially, of course. Honestly, I'm not even sure he knows I'm here."

Sully puts his mug down and cocks his head at me. He's right to question my presence, and I appreciate his protectiveness. Quickly, I amend my statement. "I'm friends with Grace, his sister. I'm kinda going through some things, and she thought this would be a good place to lie low."

"So, it is the authorities?" He gives a little chuckle.

"More like rethinking all my major life choices?"

"Ouch." He's probably rethinking this whole hospitality thing. "I think people our age are stuck between looking back and looking forward. But a little perspective and time help us learn from the past to make the future even better. I'm on a similar journey myself." His smile is kind. Understanding. I wonder what life choices he's contemplating.

We sip our hot chocolate in companionable silence, lost in our thoughts. The silence should be awkward, but it's not. Even though I just met him, he's easy to be around. His disarming smile and charm relax my usual tension. For the first time in forever, I'm at ease. It's a toss-up between this decadent beverage and this divine man as to who deserves the credit.

His phone vibrates; he looks at it and seems to consider not answering. "Excuse me, but I need to take this. If you need anything, anything at all, just call the caretaker's house number. Cell reception isn't the best." He points to the phone on the wall. I haven't seen a house phone in years, but I guess that's how things work up here.

With a nod and a smile, he answers the call. "Do you have an update on the electrical work?" I watch him walk away, and the view is incredible. Although that man may have soft hands, he has a toned body.

Sully is the complete opposite of my circle of rich men who think their money allows them to treat people as commodities. I'm done with that. I've put up with it longer than I should have for the kids. And look how that turned out. The air of mystery surrounding this reclusive mountain man intrigues me, and I hope to see him soon.

With the warmth of my hot chocolate in my hands, I admire the panoramic mountain view and let my mind wander to my future full of possibilities. This fresh start certainly has promise.

CHAPTER
FIVE

SULLY

———

I've read this page five times and can't tell you what's going on because my mind keeps wandering to Cynthia. She's far more intriguing to me than this popular biography I'm reading. What's her story? I'm adept at reading people, and Cynthia seems troubled and perhaps a little sad. I understand it all too well. The fact that she seems closed off hints at years of pushing her true feelings aside. A performance honed from necessity, not choice, is my guess. Why do I think that? It's the way she composed herself so quickly after the raccoons. From the outside, she presents a put-together, sophisticated woman, but her mysterious green eyes give her away. She seems to be seeking something. Maybe I can help her find it.

Cynthia is consuming my thoughts day and night. I can't get her out of my head. Having not seen or heard from her in two days, I'm becoming concerned. Is she okay?

Why can't I focus? Focus is one of my signature traits. Leading tech companies requires a level of multitasking and attention to detail that many people lack. I'm blessed with both. Unfortunately, they're on holiday too.

I'm a man of action. Staying busy is my addiction, and I need a fix. I need to do something. Anything other than re-read these same pages.

Decision made, I close the book and pull out my phone to research the purse sitting on my counter. After a few minutes, I determine this may prove to be more of a challenge than I thought. But I know just the person to call. I'm not above asking for help.

I text my assistant, Wendy, to get this going.

> Can you send me the number for Matt Hartman?

> Don't you usually contact your players through their agents?

Matt is the third baseman for the Carolina Reapers. He finished his rookie season and had a good showing. Wendy's right, it's a little unorthodox, but Matt's agent is my son, Julian. And I'd rather keep my children out of this for now. Otherwise, I would have started with Ashleigh. Or even Alexander. No doubt all three of them have the phone number I'm looking for. Avoiding their questions means I'll have to do this the hard way.

> This isn't Reapers-related. Number, please?

A number pops across my screen, and I start with a text.

> Hi Matt. This is Sully Decker. I need to speak to you. Please call me at your earliest convenience.

> HaHa. Very funny, Cole. Shouldn't you be enjoying your honeymoon?

I can see how he'd think this is a prank from his best friend and my new son-in-law. They're closer than friends, sharing a brotherly bond that includes a lot of playful teasing.

> Not Cole. I'll call you. Please answer the phone.

A laughing Matt answers my call. "Seriously, man, why are you calling me and not having sex with your wife?"

"Matt, I'd rather not think about my daughter in that way," I say sternly.

"Oh fuck, I mean, sorry. Mr. Decker. Shit. I thought you were Cole, and I'm sorry, I didn't mean any disrespect." Matt is fumbling over his words to apologize, and it's rather humorous. I appreciate Matt's humility. It's refreshing to see someone so accomplished remain so grounded and modest. It's one of his best qualities after being an excellent ballplayer. He's a great kid.

I let him settle before I speak. "It's fine, really. How are you enjoying your offseason?" I've always tried to keep a level of separation from my players. Being a team owner is one of my favorite jobs I've ever had, but it's a business, and I can't get too attached. However, I think Matt will be a franchise player for us for years to come. Besides, being unattached to him isn't really an option. He was the best man at my daughter's wedding last week. The lines are crossed, twisted, and blurred together when it comes to Matt and my family.

"Um, it's good, sir. I'm working out every day, following my nutrition plan, and will be ready for spring training."

I smile at how earnest he is. "Well, make sure you enjoy yourself too. Eat some holiday treats. You deserve it."

"Yes, sir, I will."

"Matt, I know this is a little unorthodox, but I need a favor. I want to contact Darcy and was wondering if you would give me her number."

"Sure, but she's right here. Would you like to speak to her?"

"That would be great. Thank you, Matt."

Darcy Davidson is Matt's girlfriend and Cole's sister. She's a designer and a very fashionable young lady. Her special touches made the wedding an extraordinary event. I'm hopeful she can help me with my dilemma.

My call with Darcy elicited several delightful girlish squeals that reminded me of my daughter. I consider calling her to check in, but she's on her honeymoon. And as Matt pointed out, I don't want to interrupt anything they may be doing. I search for other distractions and, as if on cue, the house phone rings.

"Hi, Sully. It's Cynthia. I really hate to bother you, but the dishwasher is making a funny noise, and I was wondering if you could look at it."

This is perfect. I've been looking for an excuse to see her, and here it is. The problem? I know nothing about dishwashers, but I'll figure it out. How hard can it be? I grab Dave's toolbox, hop on the ATV, and meet her at the front door.

She greets me on the porch, looking amazing in her off-white sweater and dark jeans. Her auburn hair is in loose curls, and I have an image of them spread across a pillow. Where is this coming from? I've seen hundreds of women over the years, but I've never had the image of them in bed. Ever. What is it about this woman that has consumed my every thought?

"You doing okay?" I say by way of a greeting.

"Better than the dishwasher," she says in return. "I may have killed it."

"Are you a serial appliance killer, Cynthia?" She takes pity on my poor attempt at flirting and laughs.

"I've been known to kill appliances, especially in the kitchen. They don't like me very much." I can't help my grin from spreading across my face.

"Well, killer, let me see what's going on." I walk into the kitchen and stop at the threshold. It's a disaster. Bowls, containers, and ingredients are strewn across every inch of the countertop. A fine layer of white dust coats the entire surface. Flour maybe?

"Did the raccoons break in?" It's the only logical explanation for this kind of chaos.

She rolls her eyes at me. "That would be a better story, but this is me. Making gingerbread cookies. But then it kinda got out of hand."

A chuckle breaks loose from my chest, and it feels strange. In a good way. There's something about this woman that makes me smile.

"I'm sure they are the best gingerbread cookies on the planet." At that moment, I must have made a rookie mistake because panic fills her face.

"Ohmygod, the cookies!"

CHAPTER
SIX

CYNTHIA

———

Smoke billows out of the oven and fills the kitchen. The alarm screeches, the noise deafening. I can barely see in front of me for all the smoke, when powerful arms reach around me and pull me out of danger. Yep. My baking officially crossed the line to dangerous.

The video made it look so easy. I stopped and started it multiple times, followed the instructions to the letter. And here I am, standing in the foyer, looking at a smoke-filled room, a direct result of my attempt at trying something new. I can't think of a better metaphor for my life right now. I sniffle and try to hold back the tears, but fail at that too.

"Hey, hey, no crying over burnt cookies," he says as he wipes away my tears. He holds my head between his hands, and it's intimate but also comforting. Natural. I close my eyes; embarrassment is the only thing I can focus on.

"I'm sorry. I'm a guest, and I almost burned the house down."

"But you didn't. Look at me." He tilts my head up, and I open my eyes. I'm overwhelmed by his kind, blue eyes and hint of a smirk. "There you are. It's fine. Nothing that can't be fixed. Why don't you grab a coat, and we'll go into town for dinner while it airs out."

I can't believe how understanding Sully is. Trey would've made me feel like a failure and reminded me how much my mistake would cost him. I sigh, the weight of my past falling off, little by little. I can't believe I carried it around for so long.

We head back toward the kitchen. I grab my shoes, purse, and coat while Sully opens windows and turns on the large vent over the stove. He meets me outside and checks me out from head to toe. I've traded my shame over the kitchen mishap for excitement about this adventure with Sully.

"I need to grab my keys, and then I'll drive us into town. Are you up for a little walk, or would you like a ride?" His house is down the hill, and I haven't explored the grounds since the initial raccoon attack. He motions to the large four-wheeled motorcycle thing and waits for my response.

That thing looks a little intimidating, but I think about sitting behind him with my arms around his waist and give it serious consideration. With a sigh, I subdue the tempest in my mind, choosing reason over impulse. With my luck, I'd fall off and break something.

"Let's walk. It'll be nice to get some fresh air." I take his offered arm, a warmth spreading through me as I can't stop the smile tugging at my lips.

The walk to his place is nice, quiet. I hear rushing water, and he tells me there's a waterfall on the other side of the drive. We agree to hike to it tomorrow, and the thought of the outing lifts my spirits. Again. That seems to be what happens when I'm around Sully. It's like he's my personal sunshine.

We arrive at his house, and he invites me inside while he grabs his wallet and keys. It's nice. Though not large, especially compared to the castle, the space is efficient, containing everything necessary and nothing more. Cozy. Masculine. Neat. Compared to the kitchen we just left, this one is definitely cleaner.

The dying embers glow orange and red in the hearth, casting a warm light on the stack of books next to the recliner. It's an interesting mix of biographies, a best-selling business book, and a cookbook. My curiosity is piqued. I may have discovered an authentic Renaissance man in the wild.

This house feels like Sully. Comfortable. A heavy, lingering smell of woodsmoke, sharp and slightly sweet, fills the air. Much more pleasant than the smell of burnt gingerbread. As I take in my surroundings, I'm drawn to the back wall of windows in the living room. What a stunning view! "This is incredible."

Sully throws open the glass door, and we step out onto the deck. I pull my coat around me; the wind on this side of the house is much brisker. Any amount of cold is a small price to pay for this view of the mountains. "Magnificent."

"Yeah, it is, isn't it? Enjoy the view. I'll make it quick." As he enters the house, I linger, captivated by the panoramic outlook and the quiet hum of the wind whispering through the trees. I can hear the waterfall more clearly from here, which makes me more excited to see it tomorrow.

I wish I had a camera, although a lens couldn't completely capture the feelings this breathtaking scene evokes. I consider pulling out my phone, but it won't satisfy the itch. Photography was a favorite hobby of mine, especially while the kids were growing up. With the evolution of smartphones, and as the kids got older, my hobby faded away. Maybe I'll include it as one of my new hobbies. Because baking is off the list.

Sully startles me when he joins me at the rail. "Penny for your thoughts." His smile and caring expression warm me from the inside out.

"It's beautiful here. And so peaceful. I can't imagine seeing this every day."

"Yeah, it's magical. But lonely. Sometimes, you aren't always your best company."

I can see that, especially depending on your headspace. This entire journey of self-discovery is exciting and scary, and he's right. I might not want to do this solo.

"Well, I'm glad I met you and we can keep each other company." I lean into him and knock shoulders.

He studies my face, then gives a small nod.

"That we can. Come on, let me show you what small-mountain-town life is like. It'll make you wish New York had this kind of lifestyle."

I know he was being sarcastic, but after an evening in Little Gem, he spoke the truth. I had more fun tonight in this town than I can ever remember in New York City. As we wandered down Main Street, we commented on all the holiday decor. We enjoyed the local artists and all the kitschy signs in the store windows. We laughed. And it felt good. The comfortable conversation warmed my spirit, keeping the icy mountain air at bay.

He ducks into a bakery and buys cookies to "replace the ones that gave their lives for our evening." I can't stop my blush from rising. Who needs a coat when he's warming my heart? When he asks me if I want fancy or down-home food for dinner, I don't hesitate.

"Down-home, of course! Although I'm curious about what's considered fancy here."

"Oh, fancy has tablecloths and everything. I mean, it's good, but they don't make their own butter from the milk of imported designer cows or anything."

I roll my eyes in disbelief. "I can't even," I say in a fake posh voice. He laughs at my silly joke. Whether he's actually amused or just being kind is yet to be determined. But regardless, I'll take it.

Our conversation is easy. It's like reconnecting with an old friend, even though we just met. I'm sure he's grateful for the company.

The small café reminds me of a typical New York restaurant, with its exposed brick walls and tables set very close together. When the waitress hits us with a "Y'all sit wherever you want," I know I'm not in New York anymore.

We sit at a little table by the window, and after a quick review of the menu, we both order the daily special and a glass of wine.

"Tell me about your life in New York." He's genuinely interested, but I hesitate about what I want to share. I don't want to bring down the lighthearted evening with my baggage. At my hesitation, he leans in and whispers, "I promise I won't turn you in to the authorities." And there's another wink of those blue eyes that remind me of a bright summer day. Yep. Definitely sunshine.

"Well, that's what I'm figuring out. I haven't practiced law since I got married and became a full-time mom." His eyes flit to my empty ring finger at the mention of my marriage. Is that a clue that he might be interested in me? It's been so long since I've even considered the possibility, and butterflies fill my stomach at the idea.

"A lawyer? Impressive." People usually have strong feelings about lawyers. When I think about how Trey works to hurt people with the law, I understand where the bad reputation comes from.

"I still volunteer for legal aid to help people who can't afford legal advice, serve on a few non-profit boards, but I've been thinking about doing more. I just don't know what that looks like yet. And now I need to support myself."

"It sounds like you have a heart for helping people. That's admirable."

Sully's reaction is the opposite of Trey's. Trey didn't understand why I would give my time and services away for free, but he never asked many questions, and as long as it didn't interfere with his plans, he didn't care.

With a shrug, I avert my gaze. I'm uncomfortable with the way Sully focuses all his attention on me and compliments me. I can't have him looking too closely, or he'll see how truly broken I am.

"What's wrong?"

I fidget with my napkin on my lap, unsure how to respond. "Nothing."

He leans back in his chair and folds his arms across his chest. "Not buying it. Spill." He has the look of a man who's willing to wait it out. Maybe that's what mountain life is like. He has all the time in the world. The opposite of a New York minute.

"No really, nothing's wrong. I'm not used to, well, I appreciate that you see my work as admirable."

He leans forward and puts his elbows on the table. "Of course it's admirable. Helping people, giving your time and talents, is more valuable than a job where people give their time in return for a paycheck. Don't you think that's, I don't know, significant?"

I bite my bottom lip. Do I think the volunteer work I do makes a difference? I do. There are so many people who need help and a hand up. Trey always made me feel less than, like my contributions were a silly way to pass the time. Recalling those conversations makes me angry.

The anger fuels my conviction. "Yes. Helping people is always important." As quickly as my anger boils over, it subsides. I give a little shrug. Having all the focus on me is uncomfortable, so I need to shift the spotlight.

"So what about you? Tell me more about mountain living." The look he's giving me lets me know I'm off the hook. For now.

"I love nature and the simplicity of life. I haven't been here long, but you can't beat the pace."

"Yeah, it's weird to have nothing on my calendar. Now I'm questioning whether constantly being busy is always a good thing."

"What kind of things keep you busy?"

"Oh, I don't know. Silly things, I suppose. I mean, I keep going to a book club that always has books I don't even like."

"Then why keep going?"

That's the million-dollar question, isn't it? I hate the Pretentious Book Club. Although it has a different name, Grace started calling it that, and the name stuck. Trey wanted me to attend because the other partners' wives were there, but I guess getting divorced was one way to quit.

"Because I'm the supposed-to girl." His concerned look prompts me to elaborate. With an enormous sigh, I try to explain. "My whole life, I've tried to do the right thing. All the things you're supposed to do. Get good grades. Be seen but not heard. Love your family. Honor your vows. You know, all the things you're supposed to do. But not everyone lives by those standards. Shocking, right?"

"Not really. The corporate world puts integrity in its mission statement without consideration of the actual meaning. Honestly, I'm glad I got out when I did."

"You used to work in the corporate sector?"

"Of course. I guess I was a version of the supposed-to guy for a while. College. Corporate world. Burnout. Early retirement. Now I make my own rules."

"Sounds nice. Maybe I'll work that into my reinvention." And I mean that. It sounds like he's already been down the path I'm starting.

"Who's keeping you from breaking out and making your own rules?"

The arrival of dinner and a top off of my wine glass conveniently spares me from having to answer that.

CHAPTER
SEVEN

SULLY

———

She winces, a sudden pain flickering across her face as a memory surfaces. A powerful need to envelop her in my embrace, to shield her from the world and keep her safe, threatens to consume me. What did this bastard do to her? He must have belittled her to the point she felt insignificant. The kind of man who tears a woman down to feel better about themself is trash. I have a hard time imagining this fun, vibrant woman with someone like that. Dimming her light is downright criminal.

More than once, she's mentioned reinventing herself, and I vow to help her. She needs to know she's beautiful, inside and out. On impulse, I reach across the table and take her hand. My emotions must have sent a message to my body because it's reacting in new ways too. I'm doing things I haven't done in fourteen years.

Her eyes widen in surprise. I'm not sure if it's my overactive imagination, but I swear I felt a spark. Maybe she did too?

"I don't think you need to reinvent anything. Rediscover,

perhaps. Cynthia, you're interesting. You're beautiful. Thoughtful. Intelligent. It sounds like you've been with someone who doesn't appreciate the finer things in life. And you, my dear, are fiiiiiiine." I grin and wiggle my eyebrows. I can't help but laugh as I'm rediscovering myself too. When was the last time I was remotely suggestive toward a woman? I'm full of surprises.

She looks down, shy and demure. "Thanks," she whispers. A hint of a smile graces her face, and I smile back. I can't help it. There's just something about her. I give her hand a gentle squeeze and reluctantly pull back.

Dinner is delicious, as always. This food brings me back to a time when down-home cooking was comforting, and I didn't have to worry about my cholesterol or blood pressure. But this feeling is more than the comfort food. It's the company. For the first time in years, the tension in my shoulders melts away, and I'm relaxed. A strange, calming sense of peace washes over me, and I'm intrigued by this old feeling coming back to me.

"This is so good," she says as she savors her meal. "I almost forgot food could be something other than gourmet. And I mean that in the best way." She giggles and takes a sip of wine. "I wish I had a recipe for this."

"Are you a good cook?" I question it based on the mess we left behind.

"We're here because I almost burned the house down. What do you think?" I love the snark. She's got me there.

"I think you were distracted by the handsome man in your kitchen and you forgot to set a timer."

That gets a full laugh, and I feel like I just won the World Series. Each tease brings a new blush to her cheeks and a fresh light to her eyes, making her shine.

"Oh, absolutely. Can I use you as an excuse for all my shortcomings?"

I lean in and get lost in her green eyes. "You can use me any way you want." There's a slight rumble in my voice that hasn't been there for years, and I startle myself.

Another laugh escapes her lips, and she fans herself. Not exactly the reaction I was prepared for, but I enjoy it anyway. Anything to see her eyes sparkle with life, happiness.

"Are you flirting with me?"

"Maybe? Am I that bad at it that you need to ask? It's been a while." I haven't been interested in a woman since Rebecca's death. But now I'm very interested.

"Not at all." She leans in, and I'm captivated by her. "But be careful what you're offering. I might just take you up on it."

"Check, please!" She laughs again.

After an intense showdown over the bill, I relent and allow her to pay. Damn near killed me, but it's something she's insistent about. Her need for independence outweighs my ability to pay. I can't stand in the way of her recovery and independence. She doesn't want to be beholden to anyone, and I understand that. I really respect how strong and courageous she is. This bastard really messed with her, but I'll do anything I can to build her back up.

The journey back to the house is a scenic twenty-minute drive, but it takes both hands and most of my attention to keep between the lines. Although, admittedly, there's a very large distraction in the passenger seat. My distraction seems lost in her own thoughts as she hums along to the music from my playlist. "You a big U2 fan?" I ask.

"What? Oh yeah. They were the first big concert I ever went to. I played their records until I practically wore them out." She laughs again. "Ohmygod, I'm telling my age, aren't I?"

"I'd be concerned if you called them vinyls. I still have my album collection, although I admit, I'm a fan of having all my music on my phone. It's probably my favorite use for this thing." I don't want to sound like an old curmudgeon, but I miss the days of not being tethered to the phone. Our generation's curfew was when the streetlights came on, our family had just one house phone in the kitchen, and we wrote notes to flirt with girls during class. I don't understand the younger generation's situationships, booty calls, or ghosting. In my opinion, not all things are progress these days.

"My kids used to give me a hard time about my music choices. Nothing beats sitting by the pool, listening to Tom Petty, and drinking frozen daiquiris. Now everyone is listening to podcasts and drinking Frosé. Where's the fun in that?"

I can't stop my laughter. "Tell me about your kids." She's opening up, and I want it all. I know hearing about her kids will give me plenty to work with. Until I glance over and see her lip quiver. Fuck. Fatal mistake.

I pull into the drive and stop beyond the gate. I put the car in park and turn to her. It's dark, but I can tell she's about to cry.

"Hey, hey, what's wrong?" I put my hand to her face and turn her attention to me.

"I'm sorry. Sometimes, it just hits me."

"Hey, I'm here if you want to talk. But it's okay if you don't. No pressure."

"I appreciate it. I'm just heartbroken that the kids chose their father and his new wife over me. I mean, I get why. But it still hurts."

"I'm sure it does. He's moving on…"

"Oh, I couldn't care less about him," she says quickly. Drawing a deep breath, and with a resolve reminiscent of a pitcher's final effort, she continues. "He moved on when he had his first affair twenty years ago. It's our kids. His kids, really. You see, when we got married, his wife had died, and he had three little kids, one still in diapers. I've raised them for twenty-six years. With a new family and our divorce behind him, he made it clear to the kids that a relationship with him came with access to their trust funds. So, he made them choose. Him or me. So yeah. It's my first Christmas without them." A tear slips down her cheek, and I wipe it away with my thumb. That's gotta hurt. The betrayal. Abandonment. He sounds like a master manipulator and a total piece of shit. My opinion of the kids isn't much better. I can't even imagine what she's going through.

"I'm so sorry." I brush my thumb across her cheek again, and even in the darkness, I can see her blush climb. "We can spend the holidays together. If you want, that is."

"I don't want to be an inconvenience. I'm sure you have plans."

"You're the best inconvenience. Really." I mean every word. She's exactly what I need when I never expected it. I should thank Santa for the gift of this beautiful woman coming into my life.

"Okay," she whispers. I'm about to continue our drive up to the house when she leans across the console and kisses me.

It takes a second for my brain to remember how to kiss, then my lips engage. My first kiss in years. It's foreign. It's unexpected. It's fucking amazing.

CHAPTER
EIGHT

———

I lean over and kiss him. It's impulsive, but I don't care. I don't care about what's acceptable. I don't care what people will say. I don't care about anything other than kissing this incredibly hot guy who has a heart of gold. For a moment, he hesitates. My heart leaps in my throat because maybe I crossed a line. I should have asked. But it happened so fast, and for once, I didn't over-think something.

The next thing I know, he's kissing me back, and all my worries are gone. I feel like a teenager making out in the car, hoping our parents won't find out. I feel young. Wanted. Maybe even desirable. Most of all—connected.

We break our kiss, and I sit back in my seat. I glance at Sully to find him staring at me with a look I can't decipher. Cue the overthinking. My old habits can't stay away for long. I avoid his gaze by looking straight ahead out the windshield.

"I'm sorry, I shouldn't have done that." I'm a little out of breath, but holy cow, was that kiss hot. Shit! I practically threw myself at the man. He probably thinks I'm a walking red flag. Desperate and lonely at best. All of which are true.

The deep timbre of his voice fills the car. "Why not?"

"Because…I don't know. Maybe you have a girlfriend or something."

I risk a glance his way and see the grin on his face. "I don't."

"Oh, okay. Good." I'm not sure if I'm relieved or incredibly embarrassed? Probably both. God, my face is hot.

"It was good. And I'd like to do it again. That is, if you want."

His comment, while unexpected, is very exciting. When I bite my lip, I can still taste him. His cologne isn't overpowering, but in this confined car, I'm surrounded by him. It's calming. And hot as hell. And disorienting. I can't string two thoughts together.

"Um, yeah." Way to go. Smooth as ever. I'm embarrassed to meet his gaze. Nope. Can't do it. I'm sure I'm as red as a tomato.

Sully takes that as his cue to keep driving. He takes us to the top of the hill and back to the castle. We walk in, and while the smell of smoke has diminished, it's absolutely freezing. Sully closes the windows and checks the thermostat. It's a chilly forty-two degrees in the house, but I'm still burning from that kiss.

"Why don't we go back to my place? I'll make a fire, and we'll turn up the heat here to see if we can't get this house back to a livable temperature. Go grab what you need for the evening."

I walk past the kitchen, and it's still a disaster. No elves cleaned it while I was whisked away. Yet, when I come back downstairs, Sully is cleaning it. I'm not sure how to process that. A man cleaning? Without having to be asked? Talk about hot.

"You don't have to do that," I start.

"I don't mind. Do you have everything you need? I grabbed a bottle of wine and thought we could watch a movie or something." He pauses, giving me a questioning look. "Unless you don't feel comfortable?"

"What? No. Wait, not no, I mean—yes. I'm comfortable." I face palm, groaning. "I'm sorry, I'm so awkward. I don't know what I'm doing."

"That's good because I don't know what I'm doing either." He shoots me a sheepish smile. "Let's figure it out together."

I nod. There's something reassuring about that. We're on separate journeys, but I have a feeling our paths have crossed for a reason. While this crossroad is awkward, it's also easy. And exciting. I'm not opposed to staying on the same path for a while. I'm warming up to the idea of not being alone as I figure out what's next.

We drive back to his place, and it's immaculate compared to the mess I've left. I put my hand on his arm as he turns off the car. His eyes fill with concern as he turns to me. His lingering gaze leaves me wanting more. With a brief nod, we've come to an unspoken agreement.

Let's see where this goes.

"Come on, let's get you inside and warmed up."

Like magic, he has the fire going, and the room becomes toasty and cozy, like a scene straight out of a cheesy Christmas movie. All this room needs is a Christmas tree, and it'll be perfect.

"Settle in by the fire, and I'll pour the wine." With a slight squeeze of my shoulder, he reaches to the back of the sofa and tosses me the plaid throw. He's a gentleman, always taking care of me without being overbearing about it. He's subtle, but I like it.

I tuck it around my legs and curl up, the warmth of the fire calming my nerves. The crackle of the wood and the dance of the flames are symbolic of my life situation. But somehow, this beautiful destruction has purpose. Even in this messy situation, I feel safe.

Focusing on the fire, I take a deep breath and allow myself a moment to take an inventory of the things I want to let go of. With my next breath, I metaphorically toss them into the fire.

Maybe it's my imagination, but it feels like the fire grows brighter, stronger, as it consumes my past life. It's reminiscent of a phoenix rising from the ashes.

Am I a phoenix? There's no reason I can't be.

"May I?"

I blink, pulled from my thoughts by Sully's voice. I look up and realize he's pointing to the spot next to me on the couch.

"Sure." He settles in and puts his arm around my shoulder, tucking me into his side. I slide down a little and get comfortable. The way he pulls me in to snuggle feels natural, like I'm the perfect size and shape to melt into his side. Between the fire and his body, I'm warming up quickly.

I wrap the soft cashmere blanket around him and hide in our cozy, literal cocoon. The outside world can't get us here. This layer of fabric may as well be steel armor.

"Tell me more about your work with legal aid. Is that something you want to continue?"

The fact that my crying episode in the car didn't have him running is a positive sign. Still, I lean my head against his shoulder so I don't have to look him in the eyes when I respond.

"It is. But I'm going to have to get a paying job too. When your ex is a high-powered divorce attorney, rest assured, he only made sure I won't starve, but barely. I need my own money to live comfortably in New York."

I don't want to talk about Trey. I try to shake him out of my head. "Anyway, I'd love to focus on family law and adoption."

"I think that's a noble reason to practice law. When my oldest son married a single mother earlier this year, one of the first things he did was adopt Tyler to cover all the future legal bases. Tyler is his son in his heart and on paper." I don't have to look at him to feel the pride bursting from his chest. He obviously loves his children and his grandchild.

"That's amazing. I wish I had adopted the kids when they were young, but my ex kept putting me off, saying it was unnecessary. They were my kids in every way but legally." I exhale loudly. "Then, as things got strained between us, he held the kids over my head as a weapon. If I left, I would lose the kids. So, I stayed in a loveless marriage for years. And now…"

My lip quivers, and a tear runs down my cheek unexpectedly. I quickly wipe it away, hoping he didn't notice. But given that his eyes haven't left mine, I'm not getting anything past him.

"And now?" he prompts gently.

I'm about to lay it all on the table. "And now, I'm fifty-four, starting over, unemployed, and feel like I wasted the last twenty-six years of my life. My children tossed me aside for money and their horrible excuse for a parent. I won't lie. It stings."

There it is. The root of it all. The kids choose him and the comfort money brings. I thought I had taught them better, but looking back, maybe I didn't.

These past few days, I've spent a lot of time analyzing my situation. My choices. My outcomes.

They saw what was going on over the years and how I tolerated his behavior. The saying goes, "What you permit, you promote." In hindsight, I can see that by staying for them, they thought I was okay with their father's cheating ways. I'm sure it looked like I stayed and put up with his philandering ways for the money and our comfortable lifestyle. To them, I was accepting of him and all his flaws. So why shouldn't they be okay with it? After all, he's their father.

"I'm sure it does, but maybe…well, he did you a favor."

I scoff. "A favor?"

"Well, I don't expect you to send a thank you note or anything, but I feel you'd still be in that marriage, pretending to be happy, instead of living your life. Enjoying your life. You have so much left of it to live."

He brushes my hair from my face, gives a little shrug, and kisses me on my forehead.

And I'm speechless. *A favor?*

Maybe he's right. Perhaps I should send Trey a fruit basket?

Still, the wounds are too fresh. I can't think about it in such a nonchalant way like he can. Not yet.

"Um, can we make a pact?" I say quietly.

If he's apprehensive, he hides it well. There's nothing but curiosity and a suppressed smile in his expression. He gives a slight shrug that I interpret as *keep going*.

"Whatever this is, whatever we do, can we not talk about our past? Let's focus on the present. Maybe the future is okay, but let's not talk about life before this moment."

I hold my breath, waiting for his response. Does he think I'm hiding something? Will he think I'm using him? *Am I* using him?

Then he leans over and gives me a light kiss. Well, I guess there's my answer.

And with that, we look forward. I've always heard not to trip over something that's behind you. It's a pretty wise platitude. So here we go. Starting fresh. I know it will take an effort to pack up the past twenty-plus years and pretend they didn't happen, but for now, I want to move on. To heal. And it feels like Sully wants to do the same.

I snuggle into him and feel warm from the inside out. I take another deep breath in, letting all the old feelings fill me up, and when I exhale, I let them go for the last time. Closing my eyes, I let it sink in. I feel different.

I feel *free*.

CHAPTER
NINE

SULLY

————

We talked late into the night. It was the longest first date I've ever had. We ran the gamut: movies, music, food, celebrity crushes. Our families and our pasts were off-limits. We stayed future-focused. As the fire died down, so did the conversation. Before I knew it, Cynthia was asleep on my shoulder. I extricated myself from her, tucked her in, and she curled up on the couch and slept.

I moved to the recliner and tried not to be creepy while I watched her sleep. I sorted through the million and one thoughts and feelings swirling in my head.

I didn't want to leave her, afraid she'd wake up disoriented or scared. Or worse yet, sneak out and try to walk back to Mills's house in the dark. I drifted off to sleep at some point, only to find her still sound asleep on the couch when I awoke.

For the first time in a while, I'm filled with anticipation for the day ahead. Filled with excitement and nerves, I'm like a kid waiting for Christmas. Last night, the emotions I've kept locked up for so long stretched their wings and enjoyed their newfound freedom. I understand the term mixed emotions now. I was up and down and sideways. But most of all, I was enjoying the ride.

When we kissed, I cycled through emotions so fast they blurred together. I allowed myself to get lost in the moment, and it felt, well…nice. I was surprised at first. In hindsight, I'm grateful she had the courage to just do it. Cynthia didn't give me time to worry, fret, or let my insecurities show up and overshadow the moment. She saved me from the should I or shouldn't I of that first kiss.

The fear that I'd forgotten how to kiss didn't have time to take root. There I was, in the moment. And what a moment it was! I didn't kiss her again because I want her to be comfortable. I need her to be in charge. Based on the clues I've put together, I think she needs that too. But she also needs to feel desirable. And she's definitely that.

———

I'm an early riser, so I've already made arrangements for the dishwasher repair and touched base with Wendy before Sleeping Beauty stirs. I cleared my day so I can focus on Cynthia.

Since my back is to the couch, I hear her before I see her. Her gradual waking starts with a groan and an exhale. As I slowly turn her way, I witness the most intricate morning stretch, her limbs going in four different directions but in pretzel style. Her wake-up ritual is elaborate and amusing. Based on this, I don't think she's a morning person.

"Hmmm, is that coffee I smell?" Her head pops over the back of the couch like a meerkat on high alert.

A chuckle breaks free at her antics, and I'm hopping off the barstool to pour her a cup. "Well, good morning to you too. How do you take it?"

"Light and sweet." Her morning voice is husky, and every part of me notices. It's sexy as hell.

I add that to my mental list of all the things that make Cynthia, well, her. Setting the coffee down on the table, I give her a light peck on the cheek.

"Just like you, killer." I started calling her that at dinner after the dishwasher incident. The moniker fits. Because kitchen appliances aren't the only thing she's killing. Her giggle is all the acknowledgment I need that she likes it.

She slowly sips her coffee and looks around, taking inventory of her surroundings. She focuses on the open bedroom door, the bed still made.

"Did you sleep last night?"

"A little." I'm not sure how much I want to admit.

She furrows her brow. "Where did you sleep?"

I turn my back and pour myself another cup of coffee, not wanting to see her expression when I confess. "In the chair. I wanted to be available in case you needed anything." I may have mumbled the last part of my sentence.

Arms wrap around me from behind, and I feel her body pressed against mine.

"That's sweet. Thank you."

The gesture and her proximity make me freeze. More than my heart is paying attention now, but that's my problem, not hers.

Clearing my throat, I take a moment to compose myself before turning around. I don't want her to be uncomfortable. "I'm going to take you back up so you can get ready for our outing. Are you still up for it?"

Last night, I promised her a hike to the waterfall, and the evening's light snowfall should make for a gorgeous setting. Not that I want her to be cold, but I'm hopeful she'll want to snuggle like she did last night.

"Sure, but can we take the four-wheeler thing? I'm feeling adventurous today." That gleam is back in her eye, and my heart skips a beat.

———

I raid Dave's garage for a backpack and fill it with a waterproof covering and a few blankets. I put together a light lunch and pack it away. I'll grab a bottle of wine from Devlin's when I meet my date. My date. My first date in decades. Even if I'm a different man from the last time I asked a girl out, I'm just as nervous. I check the backpack three times. And my outfit. I'm going for something that combines warmth, practicality, and "he put in an effort." This is where I could use my kids' help, but I dare not ask. I'm more comfortable in a boardroom than the outdoors, but I'll manage.

I step outside and shield my eyes from the bright sun reflecting off the snow. It's a perfect winter day. With a deep breath, I swallow my resolve and take the first step of my dating adventure.

When Cynthia opens the door, she takes my breath away. She looks like she's ready to hit the slopes in her parka and leggings, and I can't stop my smile from breaking free. It's only been three hours since I last saw her, but it feels like the first time again.

"Hi." Wow. That's smooth.

"Hi. I'm so excited. Do you think these boots will be okay?" I look at her feet, and she's wearing those furry boots that look soft and comfortable.

"Are they waterproof and warm? Can't have you getting frostbite."

"They are. Do I need to bring anything?" Her eyes sparkle with an eagerness I'm feeling too. This will be good for both of us, it seems.

"I'll grab a bottle of wine, and then we will be all set."

"Great minds," she says as she lifts a small bag with fruit and a bottle of the merlot she likes. I take her provisions and add them to my bag.

We take the four-wheeler the short distance down the drive to the trailhead. Her arms wrap around my waist, and her warm breath tickles the back of my neck. This incredible closeness tempts me to take the long, out-of-the-way route to the trailhead, savoring every moment.

When we arrive, the easy trail is cleared, with the scent of pine trees and fresh snow hanging in the air. It's more of a stroll than a hike to the waterfall, but I still offer my hand as we enter the shady winter woods. I feel a burst of joy when she takes my hand and gives it a squeeze. Even through the gloves, I feel warmer.

I'm lost in my thoughts as we walk in silence. Falling clumps of melting snow are the only sound. I'm immediately on high alert when Cynthia gasps and halts. Is she having second thoughts? Did I come on too strong? Her eyes are wide and focused on the left of the trail. A few feet away is a small bobcat, its pointed ears twitching at every sound.

I can't stop my smile as I see the delight in her eyes. "No, you can't pet him," I say preemptively. At the teasing, she bumps her shoulder into me.

"But he's so cute," she whines in a mocking voice.

"Just because they're cute doesn't mean they want to be petted."

She turns her attention to me. With a hint of disappointment and innuendo, she pokes out her bottom lip. "Well, that's a shame." She pulls her hand back from me and tucks it into her pocket.

I pinch her chin between my fingers and turn her head to look me in the eyes. "Sometimes the cute ones are the most dangerous."

Her cheeks flush, and a shy glance downward ends our intimate moment. "Are you talking about the kitty or me?"

I chuckle at her calling that wild animal a kitty. "I'm not sure," I answer honestly.

She does that thing again, where she gathers herself. I watch in amazement as her shoulders pull back and a smile fills her face. Tucking her hair behind her ear, she transforms before my eyes. The meekness drops away, and she's filled with a strong confidence that is inexplicably turning me on. I don't know if it's a "fake it 'til you make it" or a genuine rebirth, but I'll take it. More often than not, women fawn all over me, hoping to get my attention. Or my money. Cynthia has my attention without the flattery and fakeness, and I like it. A lot.

"Well, are you going to show me this waterfall you promised?"

Taken aback by her challenge, I remind her of the facts. "You're the one who stopped."

"Pfsh. I have no idea what you're talking about." She rolls her eyes and starts walking. I dutifully follow her, knowing full well this is my new default.

CYNTHIA

———

The trail opens to a clearing that sparkles in the snow and ice. It's magical. The sun reflects off the glistening snow, so bright I have to shield my eyes. Sunglasses would be helpful, but they live with the raccoons now. I could use them to hide my constant glances at Sully.

No matter how hard I try to resist, I can't stop myself from watching him. I can't help it. His facial expressions fascinate me. The crinkle of his eyes when he laughs is a network of fine lines radiating warmth. The furrow in his brow when he thinks becomes a deep crevice of contemplation. I sense the fine smile lines around his mouth are coming out of retirement. I'm confident if I asked, he'd tell me he's hard to read, that he has a poker face. However, his firm jaw, handsome face, and the glint in his eyes hint at a story I'm eager to discover.

Spinning in a slow circle, I take in all the sights and sounds of this place. A sense of peace washes over me as I breathe in the crisp, clean air, the scent of pine filling my lungs. The sound of rushing water, partially frozen, creates a dramatic focal point in the otherwise quiet clearing. I shiver, not from the cold, but from the stunning beauty of nature.

"Are you cold?" Sully drapes a blanket around my shoulders and pulls me out of my daydream.

"What? No. I'm just…It's…"

His lips curl in a knowing smirk. "Gorgeous? Stunning?"

"All of the above."

"Yes, you are."

I turn to him, eyes wide with disbelief, his words echoing in my ears. I'm far from that. Playfully, I push him away. A careless shrug, a muttered "whatever," and he returns to emptying his backpack and setting out our picnic. He clears some snow to uncover a small fire circle. With practiced ease, he prepares a fire and, as the last step, pulls a well-worn lighter from his pocket.

Patting the blanket, he signals me to sit, but I'm too fascinated by his fire-making. I can't resist asking the question that's at the forefront of my mind. "No flint and coconut husk?"

He looks at me so confused that I try to explain. "I'm a fan of *Survivor*, and they always start a fire with coconut husk. I didn't know you could start a fire with anything else." Admitting everything I know about the wilderness comes from a TV show is embarrassing, but if he wants to know me, he's got to accept some things. Like, I love *Survivor*.

His laughter fills the clearing. "I wouldn't have pegged you for a reality junkie."

Once I realize he's not laughing at my fire-starting ignorance, I relax. "Oh yeah, I love them all. *Survivor*, *The Amazing Race*, even *Big Brother*. Back in the day, I was an avid fan of *The Real World* and *Road Rules*. It's a study in human behavior."

"You think so?" He seems amused at my guilty pleasure.

"Absolutely. I've learned to read people and anticipate their reactions. It, um, well, it just makes life easier to keep the peace." And there it is. That concerned, contemplative look where he stares at me, anger simmering just below the surface. I've seen that look before. So many times before. I pull back, waiting for the lashing that's about to happen.

And then his expression changes, softens. "Hey, hey, don't be afraid of me. Ever. I'm never going to hurt you, I promise."

I nod, not out of my usual reflex, but because I actually believe him. "I know." He reaches out, and his palm cups my cheek.

"I don't know what he did to you, but I'm not him, killer." He steps back, the loss of our connection is immediate, and I'm wary. He looks to the sky and takes a deep breath.

With gritted teeth and a strain in his voice, he continues to talk to the sky. "And it pisses me off to think you have to be afraid of people's reactions as a self-defense tactic. Thinking about how you had to hide and behave to conform to, what did you call it? Keep the peace. Fucking breaks my heart." He takes another deep breath and turns away from me. He never raises his voice, but the message is clear. He's not like Trey. Not one little bit.

Sully has declared himself to be my white knight, ready to fight for my honor. He must be counting to ten to calm down because it feels like forever until he turns around.

With a determined stride, he steps toward me and puts one arm around my waist, pulling me to his chest. His eyes search mine. What's he looking for? Does he want me to argue? Deny it? I'm speechless.

His gloved finger traces across my cheek, sending a wave of warmth through my body. It's an intimate gesture, and we're fully clothed. More than fully, considering the layers we're wearing.

"Cynthia, tearing people down to feel better about yourself is for weak men. I can assure you, that's not my style. You're on a recovery journey, and I'll be here for you. Every step of the way. To give encouragement, not criticism."

After an all-too-brief kiss, he's left me stunned. He's exposed all my raw spots. Again. And while I stand here and sort through my swirling thoughts, he turns his attention to our lunch and opens the wine.

"Do you watch *Survivor* too?" He looks perplexed as he tries to follow my line of thought.

I can't help but smile at his confusion. "Because you sure know how to read people. Maybe with that and your fire skills, you could win the million dollars."

His sudden, loud laughter must scare away any animals for miles around. "No, thank you! I'll pass."

"No really, you'd be great. I bet you'd win. Hands down. You'd definitely be a fan favorite. And the prize money would be nice."

"I'm good. I don't need money." His laughter lightens as he pours the wine and hands me a plastic cup. He holds my hand as I lower myself to the blanket where he's sitting, and we both face the waterfall.

"Here's to our journey of discovery. Let's promise to keep each other honest." He clinks his cup to mine and smiles as he takes a large gulp of his wine.

We spend hours snacking, drinking, and laughing. Sully's clever, dry humor requires thoughtful consideration of his intent. I like that he makes me think. His communication has layers. He's smart and complex. And amusing.

"I want a Christmas tree." Maybe it's the wine. Maybe it's the company. But for the first time, I'm feeling hopeful about the holidays. And I want a tree.

"Okay. We'll go to town and buy one."

"No way. I'm going to get you ready for *Survivor*. You can cut down a tree, can't you?"

His eyes widen when he realizes I'm not teasing.

"Well, sure, but I think it might be better to support the local economy and..."

He trails off as I continue to shake my head no. "Nope. Come on, let's go find one and chop it down."

"Yes, ma'am," he says, his southern drawl absolute music to my ears. My smirk grows at those two little words. I'm looking forward to hearing them again.

CHAPTER
ELEVEN

SULLY

———

"Too fat. Bald spot. Not tall enough," she mumbles as we weave through the woods.

"Hey, my hair may be gray, but at least it's all there." I pull my beanie off and run my hand over my head to prove my point.

"Not you, silly. The tree." She playfully swats at my arm.

I figured that's what she was talking about, but I wanted validation.

"Oh, that's a nice one."

I flex a little, in case she's talking about my arm. She isn't. Her green eyes are fixed on the tree in front of her. She shakes the snow off the branches as she carefully examines her prize. Going through the tree checklist in her head, she nods in approval.

"Yep. This one. It's perfect." Tying her scarf around a branch to mark it as hers, she steps back, a look of smug satisfaction on her face. She wants this tree. Then I'll make sure she gets this tree.

"If you're sure," I tease. "There are hundreds of others to choose from. Or, you know, the ones grown for this purpose at the tree farm down the road." Where they have the tools to cut down a tree.

Her shoulders fall, and her eyes dim. "No, you're right. This isn't necessary. Never mind." I watch her retreat into herself, and my anger rises again as I think about the monster who did this to her. I smile and keep my frustration to myself. She's good at spotting when people are unhappy, and I need her to know I'm not mad at her, but it might take a while for her to believe that.

"I was teasing you, killer. It is ABSOLUTELY necessary that we pick out the perfect tree. I don't want you to settle ever again." I turn her gently to face me, my voice firm as I speak to her with quiet conviction. "Settling or putting yourself second is a thing of the past. From here on out, you need to live your life for you. You get what you want. Do what you want to do. The days of sacrificing your needs for others are over. Deal?"

Her eyes examine my face, looking for any sign of teasing. There is none. I'm dead serious.

"That's going to take some work," she says shyly.

"Well then, it's a good thing you've got me to help get you there." I give her a quick peck on the lips, and she reaches up and pulls me in, her mouth devouring mine. This time, I don't hesitate. My arm goes around her waist, pulling her body close. My tongue demands entry, and she responds. The kiss is hungry, needy. *Necessary.* Her hands roam my body, and she tugs on my jacket, the zipper securely keeping it in place. Her frustration builds as she makes another attempt to undress me, but the multiple layers prove to be an obstacle.

I break our kiss, and it's impossible to hold back my smirk. The cold air transforms her ragged breaths into dramatic clouds of steam, revealing her struggle. She gets an *A* for effort, that's for sure.

A shy smile plays on her lips, a hint of guilt shimmering in her eyes, as her fingers nervously fiddle with the zipper of my jacket. A zipper that foiled her plans. "Sorry, but I was just following your orders."

"My orders?" I'm loving this, but I don't recall telling her to kiss me.

"Yep." She pops the *p*, and her tongue sweeps out to lick her lips. "You told me to do what I want to do, and, well, I wanted to kiss you. Was I out of line?"

"No, not in this case. You're welcome to do that anytime." Consent is important, and I need her to know that she has mine anytime she needs it.

"Come on. Let's get you back to the house and warm you up." The fire in her kiss hinted at other ways she wants to heat things up. While I'm not opposed to that, I want her to be sure. Having sex is a big step, at least for me.

"But our tree?"

"Darlin', I think I might need a saw or some tools if you want to bring it home. I can't exactly pull it up with my hands. We'll get it later. Besides, we have things to do first."

She appears to consider my logic and reluctantly agrees.

"I guess." She shrugs her shoulders, takes my hand, and enthusiastically pulls me toward the house. We're not exactly headed in the right direction, but as long as I'm with her, I'm willing to go along for the ride.

As we make our way back to the caretaker's house, there's a concerning stream of water on the road that wasn't there when we left.

"Cynthia, why don't you go inside and warm up? Let me figure this out, and I'll be there in a minute." I quickly kiss her and give her a reassuring nod.

"Okay. I'll make some hot chocolate. It probably won't be as good as yours, but I'll try." Her smile fills her face, and the lines around her eyes highlight her happiness. I did that. I put that smile there, and I'm damn proud of myself. This feeling of satisfaction, a deep contentment blooming in my chest, surpasses even the most lucrative business deal.

Following the stream of water up the hill, I discover water bubbling out of the ground. I don't think I'll find a video online to help me here, so I FaceTime Dave to show him the problem. He remains calm as he directs me to the main valve that turns the water off to Devlin's house. Another man, Buck, joins our video call and asks me to show him various things so he can assess the situation. I was game to look at the dishwasher and attempt a repair, but I know my limits. And this is it.

Buck takes his faded Reapers cap off and scratches his head. "It shouldn't impact Dave's house, so you'll be okay. It's gonna take me a couple of days to get the equipment up there to do the full repair. You see, the pipes are close to the surface 'cause of the terrain near that house. They freeze." He shrugs and tries to explain this to me like I'm a toddler. I'm not, but I agree I'm lacking in the handyman-type things. I'm better at business deals. And baseball.

"So, they just need to thaw?" That's probably not going to happen until spring brings warmer temperatures and melts the snow.

"Naw. Could be a crack. Could be a break. Won't know until we dig it up and get a good look at it." His heavy mountain accent is so matter-of-fact. This is the way things work around here.

They don't seem too concerned about the pipes or the house, so I shouldn't be either. Except I'm thinking about its guest.

Buck says his goodbyes, and Dave fills me in on some other details about the repairs.

"Cynthia can't stay there without water," I say more to myself than to Dave.

Dave shakes his head in agreement. "No, but I'll reach out and arrange for a hotel room in town."

She can't stay in town. She just found her perfect tree.

"No, that's okay. I've got her. You worry about the house. But hey, since I've got you, can I add to my honey-do list?"

Dave's full-bodied laugh was the response I was hoping for. "Hang on." I hear the shuffling of papers and the click of a pen. "Okay, shoot."

"Let's start with cutting down a tree..."

CHAPTER
TWELVE

CYNTHIA

———

Sully enters his house, literally holding his hat in his hands. His sheepish expression warns me that something's up. "I guess everything's okay now?"

"Yeah, sure." He looks around the kitchen, a confused look on his face. "Did you find the hot chocolate?"

"Oh, yeah. I found it, but I wasn't sure how to make it, so I popped a coffee pod into the coffeemaker. I knew I couldn't screw that up." The hot chocolate he made was the most decadent thing I've ever had, and I didn't think I could do it justice. He can be the provider of hot chocolate and fire. I know my limits.

"I thought we could go into town and get decorations for the tree. Maybe grab dinner?" My law school training kicks in, and I don't think he's being totally truthful. I squint my eyes and purse my lips at him.

"What?" He reminds me of the kids hiding something from me. His eyes darting around and cheeks flushed with mischief are dead giveaways. But just like with the kids, I know I'll get the truth out of him.

"Don't gaslight me, sir. What aren't you telling me?"

He puts his hands on my shoulders and runs them down my arms until he laces his fingers with mine. "I want you to know, I'm being completely sincere," he says, his gaze intense. "It's entirely your decision. I need to tell you something, and whatever you want, I'm okay with it. You decide." What I'm deciding, I'm not entirely sure. I immediately tense up and know he's about to give me bad news.

"Sully, you're scaring me." My mind races with scenarios of things he doesn't want to tell me. Here it comes. I'm taking up too much of his time. Or he has a girlfriend or something equally devastating.

"No, no. There's nothing to fear." He takes a deep breath and lets it out. His shoulders go back, and he's at his full, over six feet, height. It's his acceptance stance. In another world, I bet he'd be an intimidating figure in the courtroom. Or the boardroom.

"So, the water is a problem. A pretty big one. And, um, I had to turn the water off."

I visibly relax. Is that all? I can brush my teeth with bottled water. I give him a "so what" shrug.

"It's going to be off for days, maybe even a week. Or longer."

The silence between us settles while my mind works to figure out what the big deal is.

"You can't stay there."

It slowly dawns on me what he's saying. My off-the-grid, hideaway-from-the-world castle is no longer a viable option. "Oh." My refuge is gone. I drop my head, the weight of defeat pressing down as I frantically sort through my dwindling options. I'll figure this out. I'm resourceful. I can do this. But deep down, the thought of leaving fills me with a profound sense of loss and despair.

Just when I feel myself beginning to heal, hopeful for my

future, this happens. Of course it does. With a sigh, I accept my fate. I'll have to leave this place. Leave Sully. I can't believe I thought that this whirlwind romance would last. My story isn't a holiday romance. It's more like *How the Grinch Stole Christmas*.

He reaches up and cups my face, his thumb caressing my cheek. "Like I said, it's totally up to you. I can get you a hotel in town. It's clean, but nothing fancy. Or I'll drive you to Charlotte if you'd rather have all the luxuries. Your call."

I shake my head at his generosity. "I'm not your responsibility. You don't have to do that." My stomach sinks a little, knowing these are my options.

"But I want to help if you'll let me. You could also, um…well, stay here if you want. I'd hate for you to miss decorating your perfect tree." His expectant gaze sparks hope in my heart once more. The tension leaves my body as fast as it came. He said I can stay! And I want to, for so many reasons. There's only one problem. I look toward the one bedroom. Is it a problem? Not for me, but I don't want this man to be uncomfortable in his home.

"I'd like to stay if you're really okay with it. I can sleep on the couch." I glance at the well-worn leather sofa. "It was comfy." Well, kinda. But beggars can't be choosers. Besides, if I stay in a hotel, I'm not exactly off the grid. Despite having a life of his own, Trey continues to meddle in mine and might track my credit card. Not to mention, I need to watch my spending.

"We'll figure that out later. I'd love for you to stay, but I want to make sure you're comfortable. Physically and emotionally."

Sully's endearing concern and caring shine through his kind eyes and reassuring presence. And it's a totally foreign concept for me to accept. After all those years with Trey, it's hard for me to believe that everything said by a man isn't manipulative and deceptive. Obviously, I need to detox from that line of thinking. Because I don't think Sully would ever deceive me.

"I appreciate the offer. Truly. I don't want to put you out." I pause, studying his face for any sign of deception. His hopeful expression makes me feel guilty about my skepticism. So I give him a slight nod. "But I'd love to stay." I bite my lip as I contemplate completing the rest of my thought. "And besides, I'm looking forward to spending Christmas with you."

His face lights up with sheer joy. "Great! Okay." He pulls me into a hug and kisses the top of my head. It's far from a romantic gesture, but it fills me with more warmth than a McDonald's coffee.

"Let's get your stuff and move you in." He pulls me toward the door, his grin stretching from ear to ear. "There's not much drawer space," he says apologetically. "But you can have it all. Whatever you need." His enthusiasm is infectious, and I'm more excited than I ought to be.

Back at the castle, I haphazardly throw my clothes into the suitcase. I toss my toiletries into another bag and quickly zip it up. Sully comes upstairs to grab my bags and loads them into my rental car to move me down the mountain to his house. Based on the case of wine in the back seat, it looks like he's raided the wine cellar. I give a nervous laugh as he tells me to "get in and buckle up" as he drives my car over the ice and down the drive. It feels like we're making a getaway, and I love the adrenaline rush.

I shoot a quick text to Grace as we drive the short distance.

> Quick change of plans. No water at the castle because of a frozen pipe. I'm moving into the caretaker's house.

> Sorry you won't be as comfortable. Proud of your adventurous spirit! He's a nice guy and will take care of you. Maybe in more ways than one? 😉

> Um...I may have kissed him.

What!?!!? OMG. That's amazing. I bet that mountain man can get freaky in the sheets. It's EXACTLY what you need. Go for it. You deserve it!

Gotta run. We're cutting down a Christmas tree today. Off to get decorations and dinner.

Indulge in dessert. You deserve it. And I don't mean the sugary kind. Love you!

CHAPTER
THIRTEEN

SULLY

———

I'm wandering around a big-box store, pushing a cart while Christmas music assaults my ears. Under normal circumstances, I'd pay someone else to do this shopping. Or skip a tree altogether. But now? Nothing could tear me away from this. Nothing. I'm on high alert, using my cart to keep Cynthia safe from the chaotic shoppers. These people are on a mission. But so am I.

Cynthia stops, puts her arms out wide, and spins in delight. "Isn't this festive?"

"Absolutely." I can't contain my smile at her childlike wonder. She's like a butterfly coming out of a cocoon, and I'm the lucky one who gets to witness her spreading her wings for the first time. It's glorious.

I maneuver the cart to block the aisle, providing a small pocket of privacy in the crowded store. I get a few dirty looks from other shoppers, but I don't care. For the moment, I need this to be about her.

Dozens of light options, a kaleidoscope of colors and brightness, hold her complete attention.

"White lights or colored lights?" She traces her finger along the shelf, pressing buttons to see what happens. Some lights change color or intensity, and one even begins playing music.

I knew she'd ask me, but this tree, this rebirth, isn't about me. This is part of her journey. I'm just a passenger along for the ride. "Which do you prefer?"

"What?" Her bright eyes fill with delight as she looks at all the choices.

"Pick what you like. This is your perfect tree, after all."

"Really?" The subtle signs all point to a life spent prioritizing others, where her own wants and needs have been consistently muted.

Most parents, especially mothers, make sacrifices for their children in big and small ways. I can't help but think about how Rebecca always ate the imperfect cookie. Or, the year the kids wanted to celebrate her birthday at a sweltering, packed amusement park. Although her birthday sacrifice was anything but peaceful, the joyful sounds of family laughter and affection more than made up for it.

Sadly, Cynthia gave up everything for a family that ultimately rejected her, leaving her heartbroken and alone.

I wrap my arms around her waist and put my head on her shoulder. "Really," I whisper in her ear. "I want this to be a killer tree." In more ways than one.

She leans into me, her back fitting perfectly against my chest. I feel her giggle before I hear it. As she pushes the buttons to turn on the various lights, she can't contain her smile.

"I've always had white lights and a professionally decorated tree because we hosted so many holiday parties. The holidays were always about business connections and making sure everything appeared perfect. I'd try to do a special kids' tree in the playroom, but even then, it was curated to match the room. But, well, it doesn't matter now, I guess." The energy drains from her as she talks about her past, while my heart breaks for her. I won't remind her she's breaking the pact, especially when I'm getting more insight into her life.

In contrast, my marriage was filled with love and mutual respect. Even as Rebecca took her last breath, whispered words of love from me and the kids filled the room. Love prevailed, even in death. Granted, I've spent too many years letting grief bury my capacity for happiness. Lately, I have realized that love and grief, like sunrise and sunset, can coexist. They aren't mutually exclusive.

"No parties, I promise. This is for your enjoyment. Pick what you want. Go overboard. No one will see it but us. And we live in a judgment-free zone."

"In that case, I want lots and lots of colored lights." There's still hesitation in her voice. I want to see her confident, overflowing with self-esteem. She deserves that. Hell, every woman deserves that. I think about Ashleigh and the Decker women, each strong and self-sufficient in their own way. Their love for the men in their lives only enhances their fabulousness. That's what Cynthia needs, and I vow to push her to put herself first for once. Starting with Christmas lights.

"Then that's what you'll have." I grab five boxes of every string of multicolored lights they have. Large bulbs, twinkle bulbs, round bulbs, LED bulbs, bubble lights, and even some shaped like chili peppers. Her eyes grow wide with amusement, and I know I hit my mark.

"Now, let's pick out ornaments. If they don't make you laugh, they can't go on the tree. No hoity-toity decorations for our killer tree." I watch her transform before my eyes; her spirits instantly lift.

"You mean no imported hand-painted ornaments that have been in the family for generations?"

"No way. I want dancing tacos and cats wearing Santa hats."

The back of her hand goes to her forehead, and she feigns

shock. "Well, I've never," she says in an all-too-believable, upper-crust New York accent.

"Stick with me and you will." I give her a quick wink and flick the pom-pom on her beanie.

A peal of laughter rings out from her, echoing down the aisle, and several heads turn our way, curious about the source of her amusement. Not wanting to cause a scene, I grab the cart and head to the next section for decorations. I see a kissing bough made of fake mistletoe and toss it in the cart. I figure it can't hurt.

After many debates about appropriate or, in our case, inappropriate decorations, we have a full cart of holiday cheer. Over dinner, we played a wild game of *Would You Rather*, both of us defending our choices with warped logic. We had everyone in the restaurant looking at us, but we didn't care. Some tables picked up the topics and discussed the choices among themselves. The restaurant was filled with our joy.

When I get the text from Dave that my list is finished, I have the green light to head home. That man has earned himself an extra-large Christmas bonus.

CHAPTER
FOURTEEN

CYNTHIA

———

The laughter and banter continue as we drive back up the mountain. Being with Sully is easy. I can drop my guard and be me, someone I haven't been in a very long time. Maybe it's because this is a fling. Maybe because he's a simple guy, living alone on a mountain, and doesn't have any expectations of me. Maybe it's because he has a heart of gold. I didn't even hesitate to move in with him, for any of those reasons or a dozen more. I also like the fact that Sully is so unlike the rich and famous crowd I know in New York. He's just a regular blue-collar guy. That I'm extremely attracted to.

"Why don't you go on in while I unload the car?" I'll add gentleman to his list of make-me-melt qualities.

As I open the door, I'm greeted by the warm air and a woodsy scent that reminds me of Sully. It's his home, so of course it smells like him. The room is softly lit by moonlight filtering through the back windows. My hand slides along the wall, searching for a light switch. Got it! The ceiling fan whirls and the pine scent fills my nose, but I'm still in the dark. Damn.

"Here, I got it," Sully says from behind me.

Several bags hit the floor with a loud thud, and the lights flicker on, illuminating the room. I must be hallucinating because there's a large tree that wasn't there when we left. Sully's hand sits at the small of my back, and he gently guides me deeper into the room. I take a tentative step and shake my head in disbelief. As I step around the sofa, I find my scarf tied around a branch.

"How?" The secure gate and single road led me to believe that we were isolated. I guess not. Who did this?

"Christmas magic." A hint of smugness tints his satisfied smirk.

"It looked a lot smaller in the woods. Um, now that I see it in the room…" I wince at my bad decision. Just add it to the list of poor decisions I've made.

"Nope. It's perfect."

I take a step closer and look at it objectively. You know what? It really is. It's just the right height with the high ceiling. I'm still baffled by how quickly someone found and set up my Christmas tree. Perhaps I'll have to accept it was Christmas magic after all.

"I thought you were over the top with the number of lights, but now I'm afraid there might not be enough."

Sully insists I take the lead in decorating the monstrous tree, though he secretly does most of the lifting and arranging. He won't let me move my scarf from that branch. He said it's part of the tree now, and I can't argue with that logic.

We admire our handiwork. Honestly, it's beautiful in a misfit kind of way. There's beauty in the chaos, and I love it more than a professionally decorated tree. It's perfectly imperfect. I snap a picture with my phone and send it to Grace. She replies with a row of heart emojis.

"Give me that," Sully says as he takes my phone from me. In

the blink of an eye, he snaps a picture of us, then kisses me and takes another picture before tossing my phone on the sofa.

His kiss is hungry, passionate. A gentle stroke of his tongue deepens it, sending a wave of heat through my body and waking up parts I thought were dead. My heart is beating like a hummingbird's wings, fast and fluttering. Our lips part, a sigh escaping mine, and our foreheads touch—skin to skin. His blue eyes close while he visibly composes himself.

He's encouraged me to be empowered, bold. Go for what I want. And I want him. The only catch is that I've never been the one to initiate sex, always waiting for my partner to make the first move. I'm not sure I know how, but I'm going to try it.

"Sully," I say, my voice surprisingly husky.

His eyes are still closed. I could be completely wrong about what's happening. I pull back, breaking our connection. His eyes snap open, his face paling with sudden concern.

"I'm sorry," he whispers. "I got carried away. I shouldn't have…"

"Stopped?" He cocks his head, obviously confused. "Maybe we could take this to the bedroom?" He swallows hard, his Adam's apple bobbing as he blinks rapidly.

"You want to…"

"Yes."

"Are you sure?" I nod enthusiastically. "Because if at any time you want to stop, you'll tell me, okay?"

"Okay, but I won't." He still looks hesitant. "Unless you don't want to…" Maybe I'm being forward, too aggressive, and am making him uncomfortable.

"Oh, I want to. It's just, well, it's been a long time."

"Oh. I know as men get older, sometimes it doesn't work…" He takes my hand and puts it on his erection. Even through his jeans, I can feel his hard length, and I rub my hand against him. He inhales sharply.

"It works." His voice is deeper, almost pained. I pull my hand away and take his, our fingers lacing together. Turning toward the bedroom, I take the first step, hoping he follows. My heart skips a beat when he does.

We step into the bedroom, then he spins me around to face him. The backs of his fingers trace down my face while he looks adoringly into my eyes. "Cynthia, you are so desirable and deserving of a perfect night. But I might be a little rusty."

My awkwardness kicks in, and any sexy comeback leaves my mind. "Do I need to get the oil?"

And he laughs. I feel the blush rise in my cheeks, and my body is awash with heat. Now is not the time for a hot flash. Although this feels different, I still have the same need to take off my clothes to cool off. But I think where we're heading is only going to heat me up more.

I reach down and grab the hem of my sweater, pull it over my head, and toss it onto the floor. Sully steps back, his eyes soaking me in. I feel exposed, but given his reaction, I'm not self-conscious about my imperfect, aging body. The cool air sends a jolt through me, and I feel the familiar hardening of my nipples against the chill.

"My god, you're gorgeous." Empowered by his words, I reach behind my back and unhook my bra, allowing it to drop to my feet.

"They aren't as perky as they used to be." This is a terrible time for my insecurities to resurface. My impulsive apology puts a hint of a scowl on this face.

"We said we aren't living in the past or talking about what used to be. Only today, remember? And what I see right now? Perfection." He uses the back of his fingers to trace my collarbone, and they trail over the top of my breasts and down my cleavage. His light touch is sensual, erotic. I may come just from his touch.

Trey never touched me like this, with reverence and devotion. Sully's soft reminder, echoing our promise, helps me chase away the intrusive thoughts of Trey. He's not ruining this for me. I've given Trey enough. I refuse to stumble over something that's behind me. And Trey is definitely behind me.

Sully and I agreed to live in the moment, and what a moment this is.

We take our time undressing one another. With each piece of clothing that hits the floor, we uncover the once-hidden skin. With our hands, with our mouths. I thought these moments only happened in movies and romance novels. At fifty-four, with a thrill coursing through me, I'm finally having my main-character moment, and it's a feeling like no other. Is this what I've been missing all my life?

I unbutton his flannel shirt and slide it off his shoulders. He lifts his arms and lets me pull his T-shirt over his head, my fingers trailing up the side of his chest. He's fit, his body lean and hard, with not a single soft spot suggesting a potential "dad bod." I pop the button of his jeans and slowly drop the zipper. His hand, large and strong, covers mine; his touch a silent but firm stop.

"Not yet, beautiful." He leads me to the bed and coaxes my leggings down. I try to remember what underwear I've got on, but I can barely compose a coherent thought. My brain's off, and my body's in charge now. I just want to feel. Let the past go. Focus on the present. And enjoy what's happening now.

CHAPTER
FIFTEEN

SULLY

———

I'm so hard I can barely function, but I'm glad to know the old guy has risen to the occasion. I focus my attention on Cynthia. Her wants. Her needs. While we said no past, it's obvious to me her ex made her feel "less than" when she's anything but that. She's smart. Beautiful. Funny. Her body is incredible. The softness of her curves, the silken touch of her skin, and the constellation of freckles on her body have me mesmerized. Her beauty is captivating, demanding a thorough and dedicated appreciation.

I guide her down onto the bed and join her there. As we lie side by side, my hand traces her hip and slides back up to explore her breast. The sensuality hangs heavy in the air as she drinks me in with her emerald eyes, their intense green seeming to absorb my very being.

I'm not in a rush. I'm not a college guy, thrilled he's getting laid. No. I'm mature now. Appreciative of the connection we share. Mature enough to acknowledge her vulnerability. This isn't a romp in the sheets for her, and I won't treat her like it is.

The Christmas tree's lights filter in from the other room in a warm, kaleidoscopic glow, the light shifting and dancing across the walls, creating a magical atmosphere. It all feels surreal.

"You." I kiss her neck. "Are." A kiss to her collarbone. "Stunning." I take her nipple into my mouth and feel her arousal with my tongue. Her hands continue to touch my body in a slow and methodical way. We're both taking our time, savoring each other.

I'm rewarded with a moan that almost makes me come in my pants. Shifting my attention back to her, I continue to explore her body with my mouth. When I reach her panties, I look up to make sure this is still what she wants. When she reaches down and slides them off her body, that's all the validation I need. I waste no time kissing down her hip to worship every inch of her.

We explore each other's bodies, tentatively at first, then with growing confidence. Me with my mouth, her with her hands. Her fingers trace up my neck and rake through my hair, her nails gently running over my scalp and sending tingles down my spine. It's almost enough to distract me from my mission. Almost.

I lick and suck at her until I know I'm about to hit the jackpot when she arches her back and grips my hair in her fist. I can't suppress the smile that crosses my lips and am encouraged to continue my mission objective. I won't stop until she orgasms on my face. Working her with my tongue and fingers, I'm rewarded with my prize. There it is. A pulsing of her walls and a sound so sensual that it should come with a warning label.

I work my way back up her body, stopping to say hello to her hardened nipples, but never taking my eyes off her angelic face. When she opens her eyes, she scrunches them at me.

"Well, that was, um, well, I don't quite have the words." Her voice is gravelly, almost strained. I give myself a mental fist pump. I did that to her. I mean, it's been a long time. A seriously long time. I haven't been with anyone since Rebecca, and when I'm hit with a twinge of guilt, the soft caress of Cynthia's fingers brings me back to the moment. I'm not cheating. I've mourned long enough, and Rebecca wouldn't want me to continue my lonely existence.

With a slight chuckle, I whisper in her ear, "I didn't think you could get any more beautiful, but the curve of your neck and flutter of your eyes when you come are the most incredible sight I've seen."

She playfully pushes me away. "Would you stop?"

I brace myself on my elbows, silently grateful for the planks I do each morning. Keeping my weight off her and creating a slight space between us, I try to figure out what she's thinking. Is she playing? Serious? Uncertain? Does she really mean it?

"Do you want me to stop?" I don't think she does, but I will if that's what she wants. I'd do just about anything she wants. The blush fills her cheeks, and she turns her head to the side. Her teeth bite into her bottom lip as she decides what she'll share.

"No, of course not. It's just, well…" I shift to the side and lie on the bed beside her, my eyes finding hers. I take her hand in mine and weave our fingers together. I want her to feel comfortable. And I want to know everything about her. Including her desires and needs.

"It's okay. You can talk to me. You're safe here. I promise." My fingers have a mind of their own, and they brush her hair back from her face. Her neck turns red, a deeper blush fills her face, and she turns to hide in the pillow. A nervous energy is coming off her in waves, and I pull away, giving her space to collect her thoughts and speak.

"I know. I'm not used to this."

"This?" I do my best to stay neutral, but my erection is demanding attention. He'll just have to wait. I shift my weight, trying to ease the pressure, a slight relief washing over me.

Cynthia is on a healing journey, and being able to express her wants and needs is a big part of that. At least I think so. I'm not a therapist or anything, but she certainly deserves to be respected. Listened to. *Loved.*

With an enormous sigh, she lifts her face to mine. My concern washes away, and the smirk I've been hiding shows. She responds with her own shy, adorable smile.

"Are you for real? I'm not used to this, this, well, this flattery. And attention. I think you're serious, but it makes me uncomfortable. I don't know how to respond." She buries her face in the pillow again.

I gently touch my palm to her cheek to get her to look at me. The bright-green eyes that I've seen light up at the sight of silly decorations are now clouded with a heavy apprehension, their usual sparkle gone. I lean down and kiss her tenderly. My heart aches knowing someone stripped this beautiful woman's confidence and sass. I vow to bring that back for her sake, more than mine.

"Killer, I mean everything I say to you. You're smart, funny, and extremely desirable. Not to mention tasty." I lick my lips as a reminder. "But more than anything in this world, I want you to feel that deep in your bones. I want you to glow from the inside out, not for me, but for you. Most of all." I take a pause, watching her eyes grow with anticipation for my words. I gently rest my forehead against hers, the soft touch a silent communication, giving her time to understand.

"Most of all?" She's waiting for me to finish my thought. I close my eyes and leap.

"Most of all." I swallow and pause. I pull back and gaze longingly into her eyes. My hands go to her, and I pull her in. I'm done fighting it. "Most of all, I want you to feel what it's like to be truly and deeply cared for. The open and honest communication. The respect. The comfort it brings your soul, knowing there is one person on this earth who longs for you. Desires you. In every way. You're an amazing woman, Cynthia, and I need you not only to hear it, but to believe it."

Tears well in her eyes, one escaping and rolling down her cheek. I kiss it away. My goal was not to make her cry and ruin this intimate moment, but here I am.

"I'm sorry, killer. So sorry. I never meant to hurt you," I whisper.

CHAPTER
SIXTEEN

CYNTHIA

———

I glance at this amazing man and his wounded look. How did I manage to do that? Leave it to me to mess up this beautiful thing we have. With a furrowed brow, he pulls away. That's not going to happen if I have a say in it.

"Sully, don't you dare." My voice is practically raspy. Emotions wash through me, leaving me in a tangled mess, but the one thing I know for certain is that this man is a treasure, and I will cherish him. His kind heart and caring nature are like nothing I've ever experienced.

Whether it's the outburst, my tone, or my words, he freezes his withdrawal. I snuggle back into him and wrap my leg over his hip. I'll hold him down if I have to.

"You aren't going anywhere until I say so." I have no idea where this newfound boldness comes from, but Sully seems to like it, judging from the wide, almost mischievous, smile stretching across his lips. Yes, starting sex is new for me, but communicating like consenting adults about sex is mind-blowing. I've definitely never done this.

So I'll take some of the blame for my lackluster sex life. But there's something about Sully's openness that makes me want to tell him exactly what I want. And how I want it. Where I want it.

"I want you to fuck me senseless. After my introductory orgasm, I'd like another. Please." The words die on my lips, and I wince at my vulnerability, the boldness that fueled my request evaporating. His response? He laughs. A full belly laugh. He strokes my face and kisses me on the nose. It's not exactly the reaction I was aiming for.

"Gah, killer is the right name for you. 'Cause, woman, you are killing me." He pulls me in tight and on top of him.

I lean down and kiss him, claiming him, marking him as mine. His erection is still covered by some inconvenient underwear, but it doesn't stop me from grinding on him until I'm about to come again. I'm dry-humping him like a virginal teenager. But I don't care because the pressure on my clit and the silky feel of his boxers are doing it for me. Maybe it's just been a while, but this erection I'm rocking on seems so much larger than Trey's, and my excitement intensifies. I can't wait to find out how he feels inside me.

My hormones rage, and if I were twenty years younger, I'd want to have a baby with him. Right now. I mean, if I had working ovaries, they'd be aching. Anything to stay naked and make me feel this good. I haven't been this horny in ages, and it's making me feel youthful.

His hands rest on my hips as I ride out my orgasm. My scrambled brain makes it hard to form a coherent thought. I'm not upset as his satisfied chuckle fills the room. I get the impression he enjoyed that too. Even though my body feels like a limp noodle, I want to take care of his ever-present hardness growing between us.

His hand catches mine as I move to remove the last barrier between us. He stops it, his fingers gently brushing mine, before bringing it to his lips for a light kiss. He settles our joined hands on his chest, his heartbeat a steady rhythm against my palm.

"We need to talk."

My heart stops at the seriousness of his tone. "That's never good."

I relax into his sweet and tender kisses as he pulls me to him so we lie side by side—eye to eye.

"No, no, it's fine. I want to talk about what's next, your boundaries, and let you know I don't have any protection here. When I say it's been a long time, I mean decades."

I let out a sigh of relief. It's been a long time for me, too, and I've never been with someone mature enough to stop and talk about it. It used to be that we rushed into things, and I'd have worries and regrets after. This is actually refreshing. If not a little frustrating. I'm ready to finish what we started, but apparently, he's willing to slow us down. To talk. I do my best not to roll my eyes.

"If this is the *are you on birth control* talk, you don't have to worry about that. Between age and a hysterectomy, I won't be getting pregnant. And after all the affairs I lived through, I was getting tested regularly. But that was years ago. Which was also the last time I found myself in this situation." I reach between us and grab his hardness, and he's still ready to go. Good to know.

His smile widens when I rub my hand up and down his length. "And while I appreciate you wanting to set boundaries, I think we're past that. I don't have any boundaries. I want you to fuck me. Do with me as you will. My body is yours."

A low murmur fills his chest, and he looks to the ceiling. "I'm a bit rusty…"

"So you said, but I did offer to get the oil." My sudden sass surprises me, but he seems to find it amusing. "Would you rather not have sex?" I realize maybe he's the one who's uncomfortable.

"Oh, I want to, just need to manage your sexpectations."

"My sexpectations?"

"Yeah, I'm not sure how long I'll last, so I don't want you to be disappointed." He's thoughtful, even in this awkward, almost-having-sex, time. It's endearing.

"Oh Sully, you can't disappoint me." Before I finish my sentence, he's on top of me, his underwear quickly discarded, and the tip is right there at my entrance. He looks at me and, without hesitation, I grab his ass and pull him into me. I don't want gentle. I want it hard and fast. And wow. Let's just say he understood the assignment.

We're snuggling in a post-orgasmic bliss, both quiet but content. His fingers play with my hair until I hear his gentle snore next to me. I want to stay here forever, hidden from the world and my past. Why can't this be my present and my future? I can picture it now. He can fix things at the castle, and I can, well, have sex with him. I like that idea.

I struggle to untangle myself from Sully's long limbs. I move, and he pulls me tighter to his side. "I have to pee," I whisper. He releases me without a word, a sly smile on his face. I put on his soft flannel shirt, his scent embracing me like another hug. His shirts are mine now. Sully will just have to go shirtless from here on out, and I certainly won't mind.

I freshen up and take a long, hard look at myself in the mirror. My normally tamed, soft waves are curling now, and my face has a glow I haven't seen in a long time. I hardly recognize the reflection in front of me. I'm not polished and put together. I'm makeup-free. I'm wearing a man's barely buttoned shirt. I'm freshly fucked. And I feel beautiful. For the first time, I feel… enough.

While he sleeps, I curl up on the couch, gazing at our charmingly imperfect Christmas tree. Its uneven branches have way too many lights. The ornaments dangle precariously, threatening to fall to the floor at any moment. But my scarf is a reminder that I picked this tree, and even with its flaws, it's perfect to me.

I mull that thought over, thinking about myself and my life. Sully sees me differently from how I see myself. Maybe I am beautiful to him, just like this tree is the most spectacular tree I've ever seen. My heart flutters and my stomach flips as I think about him. Certainly, I'm not falling in love with him this quickly. It's too soon. What will people say?

As I close my eyes, I hear Sully's simple mountain wisdom play in my head. He's right. Fuck those people.

CHAPTER
SEVENTEEN

———

Our days are filled with fun and laughter, and our nights are just as entertaining. We've hiked and ridden the four-wheeler. Successfully made delicious gingerbread cookies. Shopped in town. Snuggled on the couch watching John Hughes movies. Danced under the Christmas lights. And had sex. Plenty of sex. Enough that I've knocked the rust off and feel like I'm back in my prime. Well, almost.

I feel alive again. Cynthia's spirit has revived me, bringing me back to life. I don't want to let her go, but after Christmas, I have obligations. Eventually, we'll have to talk about our lives outside of this bubble. But I'm okay putting it off a little longer.

Cynthia insisted on going into town on her own today. I hate her being away, but the roads are dry and clear, and I can't smother her. She needs some personal freedom. I use this time to catch up on business and make a quick call to Alexander to check on his family.

"How's Dani?" I'm certain Alexander isn't letting his pregnant wife do anything strenuous, especially with her due date a few weeks out.

"She's glowing like sunshine. The doctor said she's doing great. She doesn't like the naps I'm making her take, but she and Tyler use that time to snuggle, which makes her happy. And sad. I'm telling you, the hormones are no joke."

I can't help but laugh at my overprotective son. He's about to learn the hard way that you can't plan anything with children or pregnant women. "And how are you?" I know how he worries and is always the caretaker.

"Good. Good. Ready. I'm worried about Dani, but she assures me she's done this before, and she'll be okay."

"For once, let her take the lead on this one. Trust me. Let her hit you, call you names, squeeze your hand until it breaks. Women are incredibly strong. And Dani's resilient. She's got this."

"Yeah, you're right."

"Listen, I'm calling for a favor."

"Of course. Is everything okay?"

"Yeah, yeah, I'm fine." I can't stop the smile when I think about Cynthia and her *it's fine even though everything is burning down around her* attitude.

"I need to know about the law firm you used when you adopted Tyler. Was it local to Charlotte?"

"Jack Manning found them for me. They have an office in Charlotte, but they're based out of New York, I think. Why? Am I about to get another sibling?" Curiosity fills his voice.

"No, you three are all I can handle. I'm asking for a friend. That's all. I'll call Jack. Nothing for you to worry about." Jack is Alexander's old college buddy and the Reaper's general counsel. I hate to bother him during his time off, but I send a quick text with my request, and he responds almost immediately. No questions asked.

The sound of a helicopter landing close by spurs me to

bundle up and go outside. I hop on my four-wheeler and weave around the waterline construction. I wave at Buck as I pass his crew working on the massive hole they've created and arrive at the helicopter pad to greet my visitors.

Once the blades slow, the door opens, and Matt helps Darcy out of the cabin. Darcy skips toward me and gives me a hug. Matt extends his hand, and I pull him into a half embrace, slapping him on the back. I'm feeling extra emotional today. "Good to see you two. How was your trip?"

"It was amazing. Thank you for everything. We had the absolute best time," Matt says as he puts his arm around Darcy. He smiles at her, an obvious remnant of a memory in his glance. The City of Lights and Love will do that to a guy.

"Yes, thank you, Mr. Decker," Darcy says. "You spoiled us with private jets and five-star hotels. It was a very generous gift."

"Speaking of gifts, was your mission successful?"

Darcy's eyes light up with excitement. "It was the most extravagant and posh experience, but your checkbook opened doors and, with that persuasion, I was able to get exactly what you wanted. They let me know it was 'quite irregular,' but they did it anyway. And I took care of all the Decker girls, too, just like you asked."

"Excellent. Um, where is my package?" I'm eager to get it back to the house and hide it from Cynthia.

"Ohmygosh, hold on." She runs back to the helicopter and returns with an ornately wrapped box. "I figured you'd want it gift wrapped. I hope that's okay."

"More than okay. I can't thank you enough. And I appreciate the delivery service too."

"Are you kidding?" Matt says with a sense of wonder. "This was the coolest thing ever. I'd give up baseball to be your delivery guy anytime."

I can't hide my smile. These kids give me hope for the future. They're the best kind of people, always ready with a kind word and a helping hand. I'm grateful they're part of Ashleigh's life. And I'm a pretty lucky team owner to have a kid like Matt on the Reapers.

"You're much more valuable to me on the field, but I'll keep you in mind if I need another big errand."

I glance at my watch to see how much longer until Cynthia returns. "Would you like to come in for some hot chocolate? My house is still out of commission, but I'm staying down the road at the caretaker's house."

"We appreciate it, but we need to head back. We're going to Charleston tomorrow for Christmas, and this one has to wrap all the gifts she got in Paris," Matt says with a wink at his girl.

I hold the box tight. "Thank you again. I really appreciate it."

"Absolutely." Darcy steps forward and stretches on her toes to give me a kiss on the cheek. "I can't wait to meet her. You seem different, in a good way," she whispers. I feel the warmth rise in my cheeks against the cold air. I give her a slight nod. She's right. I am different.

"Merry Christmas!" Matt shouts over the noise of the blades beginning to whirl. He helps Darcy into the helicopter, and they take off, waving goodbye.

I rush back to the house and hide the gift in the storage room off the balcony. I'll have to figure out a way to make this a non-Christmas gift.

Our gift exchange issue was contentious, and Cynthia pulled out her courtroom skills on me. We negotiated and compromised. We agreed that each can spend one hundred dollars any way they want on gifts. And not a penny more.

I admire her determination to conserve her money and work toward independence, and I refuse to stand in her way. It's part of her journey, and I'll do what I can to help. Like the call Jack is making for me. I'm not giving her anything, just making a connection. The sense of accomplishment she gains from achieving her goals will fuel her confidence.

Cynthia was insistent on going into town by herself today.

I'm sure she's still shopping since I haven't heard from her. It worked out great, so I didn't have to make an excuse for Matt and Darcy's visit.

Rather than a few expensive gifts, I opted for quantity over quality, giving her lots of smaller, less expensive items. While I'm worried about her reaction to my breaking our agreement, I began this project well before we shook hands on it. Besides, it's not really a Christmas present. At least that's going to be my defense when the time comes. And it will probably come.

Not sure if it's the anticipation or guilt, but I jump in surprise when Cynthia opens the door, laden with grocery bags. "Did I see a helicopter up here?"

"Probably just sightseeing or something. Here, let me get those." I take the bags from her and put them on the counter. "What's all this?" I peek in the bags and find all the ingredients for a holiday meal.

"Well, since we've been doing online cooking lessons, I thought I would graduate to a Christmas roast. The butcher's wife was very kind and wrote the instructions for me and even gave me her number in case I ran into trouble." She lets out a gigantic sigh. A content sigh. "I love it here. Everyone is so nice." She unwraps her scarf and hangs her coat next to mine by the door while I unpack the bags. Seeing our coats side by side just feels right.

"I've been trying for weeks to convince you to leave New York and move here, but it's the butcher's wife who convinced you to stay? Good to know where I stand," I tease her, and she throws her hat in my direction.

"Well, she has the best meat." She shrugs like it's the end of the discussion.

"I thought you liked my meat?" I pretend to pout and poke my bottom lip out.

She snakes her arms around me and slides her hand down my thigh, grabbing my cock and giving it a wake-up squeeze.

"Eh, it's all right, I guess." Her sweet, melodic giggle serves as my aphrodisiac.

I wrap my arms around her, pull her tight, and whisper in her ear, "Darlin', I'll fuck the sass right out of you."

"I dare you."

Challenge accepted.

CHAPTER
EIGHTEEN

CYNTHIA

———

I roll over and reach for Sully, only to find cold sheets and an empty bed. The disappointment hits me hard. The subtle sounds of his light snoring and the rough texture of his morning stubble against my skin have already altered my view of mornings, even after just a few weeks. And the slow, tender morning sex. In the morning, Sully is a picture of gentle affection, a world away from the intense, almost-feral nighttime Sully who leaves me satisfied but utterly spent. And exhausted.

I stretch my body, the slight irritation between my thighs from his stubble a reminder of the way he tied me down and didn't stop licking and sucking until I came on his tongue three times. The smirk on his face and glimmer in his eyes when he proudly announced he'd hit a triple will be a cherished core memory. Afterward, he fucked me so hard, with what he called "the ultimate grand slam." His name was the only word that passed my lips for minutes afterward. He sure warmed up from someone who called himself rusty.

Maybe it's the mountain air, but I suspect my improved sleep is because of the man currently missing from my bed. The delicious aroma of coffee and bacon finally chases away my typical morning grumpiness, bringing a smile to my face. Reaching the bathroom, I look in the mirror and laugh at the person staring back. I'm a mess. My hair is in a haphazard bun, barely brushed, and I haven't put on makeup in weeks. Yet there's a healthy glow that makes me feel beautiful. Happy.

I slip into one of Sully's soft flannel shirts, and love that it still smells like him. I wear his shirts so frequently, they might as well be mine.

When I walk out of the bedroom, Sully's blue eyes darken, and for a split second, I fear I've done something wrong. Old habits die hard. But the smirk on his face shows that he's anything but angry. Torn between a morning kiss and coffee, he makes the choice for me, striding toward me and embracing me in a long, hungry lip-lock.

"Good morning to you too." I can't stop the girlish giggle that escapes my lips. I've been doing that a lot these days.

"Merry Christmas, killer." He sweeps an errant strand of hair from my face and tucks it behind my ear.

OMG. It's Christmas. Several weeks ago, I wasn't sure I'd even acknowledge the day; the sadness of not being with my family was just too raw. But now, here with Sully, it's like he's my new family, the one who's picked me. That's one of many things I love about him. And there it is. I'm falling in love with this sexy, reclusive mountain man.

"Merry Christmas to you too. Smells like you're up to something." Despite the incredible kiss, my attraction to bacon is unwavering.

With a chuckle and peck to the top of my head, he turns his attention to the stove. "I thought we'd have a proper breakfast before we tackle your Christmas roast."

I'm starting to regret bragging about making a special meal. I'm an absolutely terrible cook. Luckily, Sully is decent in the kitchen, or I would have starved up here. I've enjoyed the little cooking lessons he's given me, but I don't think they're enough to pull off a big dinner. Self-doubt creeps in like a long-lost friend.

"Yeah, it's probably a good idea to eat now, just in case." I may have mumbled it, but based on Sully's sudden change in demeanor, he heard me. His face goes from carefree to stern in a flash, creating a sudden chill in the air. Was it something I said?

He aggressively turns the knobs on the stove, and the flames extinguish with a whoosh. He turns toward me and focuses his steely gaze in my direction. I have another quick image of him in a sharp, dark suit, his voice resonant as he commands the board-room. I tuck that fantasy away for later. This side of Sully is intimidating and a little scary. Not that I'd ever imagine him hurting me, or anyone else, for that matter. But I can picture him getting what he wants with that glare.

"Don't." It's just one word. Firm. Serious.

I'm not sure what triggered him, but I'm sincerely confused. "Don't what?" I ask meekly.

"Don't put yourself down. This world is full of people who will gladly do it for you. As I'm sure you're well aware." Fire burns in his words, but what he's not saying is white hot. He's talking about Trey, without knowing him or even his name. His jaw ticks as he takes a calming, deep breath. With a gentle touch, he reaches out and caresses my face.

"I didn't put myself down." I bow my head, unable to look at him. His finger below my chin raises my head, encouraging me to look him in the eyes.

"You did. And I know it'll take a long time to heal from those wounds, but please stop picking at the scars. You're amazing and can do anything you put your mind to. I know that for a fact. You're going to make the best Christmas dinner I've ever had. Of that, I have no doubt. And I need you to be certain as well."

Tears form in my eyes, and I can't stop them from falling. I don't think anyone has ever believed in me like this. He supports me with his whole being. And just like that, his powerful arms wrap me in a loving embrace, and I'm immediately filled with self-confidence. I can do anything with this man by my side. And that includes making a delicious dinner.

With my head buried in his chest, I say the quiet thing out loud. "I love you." He tenses up, and I fear I've said the wrong thing. I try to pull out of his embrace, but I'm locked in his arms. I'm not going anywhere until he allows it.

He kisses the top of my head, releases me, and begins plating the food. Well, that's not exactly how I thought this would go, but I won't backtrack. Not taking it back. Nope. I feel something for Sully that I've never felt before, not even with Trey. The connection is hard to explain. Gratitude, affection, sexual satisfaction, and contentment swirl together to create this feeling. Most of all, I'm a better person because of him. So even if he doesn't feel the same about me, I'm okay. You meet people for a reason or for a season. Sully may be one or both. Only time will tell. Regardless, I'm a stronger woman because of him. Of that, I'm absolutely certain.

CHAPTER
NINETEEN

SULLY

———

Well, Thomas Sullivan Decker, you royally fucked up. This incredible woman confesses her love, and you reply by asking if she wants extra bacon.

Did my response deal another blow to her already damaged self-esteem, leaving her feeling exposed and vulnerable? I'll never know because she's incredibly gifted at shielding her wounds. My chest tightens thinking about my carelessness.

Of course I have feelings for her. They snuck up on me and then consumed me like a hungry fire. But I have other feelings I need to settle.

She cleans off the table, going on as if I didn't make this special day awkward. I nervously clear my throat.

"Um, I need to run up the hill to do something before we start dinner. Are you okay for a little bit?"

Her movements freeze for a fraction of a second, then her practiced smile fills her face. "Of course. You don't have to babysit me, you know?"

I curse myself. How could I be so insensitive? I'll make it up to her. I have to. I absolutely refuse to be categorized with her ex, a man who clearly lacks the vision to see this beautiful and extraordinary woman for who she truly is.

Wrapping my arms around her, I pull her tight, kissing her behind the ear. Even if she's upset, her body responds with red rising up her neck. I'm captivated by the involuntary blush that creeps across her pale skin when I touch her.

"Have I told you how damn sexy you are in my shirt? Promise me you won't take it off today." Her head gives a slight shake. She doesn't believe me. "Promise me. Until I take it off you. I want to unwrap you like a Christmas present and play with you all day."

A sly smile accompanies another disbelieving shake of her head.

"You're incorrigible."

"More like insatiable when it comes to you. I need you to promise."

"I promise." She turns in my arms and seals the promise with a kiss.

———

The cold temperature in my house doesn't extinguish the burning I have for the woman I left down the hill. But I need to do this. I need to talk to Rebecca. Fourteen years have passed since she died, yet I still find myself speaking to her, though less often now. The silence in the house is heavy with memories.

The spot my wife cherished pulls me to it. Rebecca's smile stares back at me from the sea of family pictures on the grand piano. I sit on the bench and place the framed picture of us on the music shelf.

Rebecca played the piano beautifully. Her fingers would float across the keys and fill the room with music. When the kids were younger, we'd gather around this spot and request her to play songs. We'd try to find a song she couldn't play. We never did. She tried to teach me to play, but the best I could do was the melody in "Heart and Soul." My fingers absently move over the keys, and I can almost feel Rebecca beside me, playing her part.

"Hey, Becks," I whisper. "I wanted you to know I found someone, just like you wanted me to." I keep playing the song on repeat, the simple tune echoing in the quiet house. "It took me a while. But she's special. You'd like her." My hand moves from the piano keys to the framed picture, the silence deafening. I run my finger over her face, remembering the love and life we had together. "Thank you for teaching me how to love. What we had was special, but it's time to, well." I swallow hard, dislodging the lump in my throat. It shouldn't be hard for me to say, but it's like acknowledging this chapter is over. And I need to tell Rebecca.

"I love her, Becks." As the words quietly leave my lips, I know this is the real deal. "I love Cynthia," I say with more conviction. "But that doesn't mean I love you any less. I could never. Everything good in my life is because of you. Everything. Honestly, I wouldn't be surprised if you were involved in this somehow." A tear escapes and slides down my cheek.

As I close the piano lid, I look outside and see a chipmunk on the deck watching me. I swear it's grinning.

"Yeah, yeah. I hear ya."

I grab a few Christmas movies, and before I leave, I put the picture back in its place. "Love you, Becks."

———

When I get back to the cabin, Cynthia has a video of Gordon Ramsey playing on the TV. And as promised, she's in my flannel shirt. Now, her hair is clipped back, and she's furiously chopping something. It's a little terrifying.

"Hey, killer, I'm back. You started without me?"

She glances over her shoulder at me and returns to chopping, the knife hitting the chopping board aggressively. "Yeah, I didn't know how long you'd be, so I wanted to get it started."

I'm flooded with guilt again. Her walls are up because of me, and I need to tear them down. Right now.

"Hey, do you mind putting the knife down and joining me in here for a minute? I need to tell you something." I sit on the couch and pat the spot next to me. Reluctantly, she takes it. I pull her to my side, wrapping my arms around her.

"I know we said no past, only present, but I'm going to break that rule." She tenses up in my arms and shifts her weight away from me. "No, it's okay. Let me explain my reaction to you saying you love me."

She tries to pull away again, but I won't let her. "You don't have to," she says.

"Actually, I do." Hoping to reassure her, I give her a gentle kiss on her soft lips.

With a deep breath, I begin my story. "I was married to Rebecca for over twenty years. She was the love of my life. We were the couple that others envied. It wasn't always perfect, but it was pretty damn close. So, when she died fourteen years ago, a piece of me died too. I distanced myself from everyone, even from my children. I've never dated or even been with a woman since then. When I told you it's been a long time, I meant it."

She turns her body to me, her eyes full of empathy and understanding. Her hand cups my face, comforting me. I find it easier to continue because of her kindness.

"Cynthia, you captivated me from the moment I met you fighting off the raccoons." We chuckle at that memory. "You're fierce, resilient, funny, and so damn gorgeous. Being with you these past few weeks has brought me back among the living."

"I'm glad. You've been good for me too."

"It's just that you caught me a little off guard with your, well, declaration. Not that my heart didn't skip a beat when I heard it —because it did. I just needed to tell Rebecca goodbye."

My hand brushes her hair away from her face. Her eyes grow wide as she catches what I'm throwing. She moves to straddle my lap, and I can feel her anticipation waiting for my next words.

"Cynthia, I love you too."

CYNTHIA

———

He loves me. He not only told me, but he showed me. His hands touched my body like it was the first time, seemingly in awe of every bump and blemish. And after two orgasms at the mercy of his fingers, I'm spent. This man is going to kill me, in the best way. We certainly aren't teenagers, but our sexcapades make me feel like one. Even our time together cuddling while we watch sappy Christmas movies warms my heart more than a raging fire.

We're lying on the rug next to the Christmas tree, out of breath, but not in any hurry to leave this spot.

His finger lightly traces against my skin, and I close my eyes, savoring the gentle touch. The lights from the Christmas tree create a chaotic dance of colors, and it's exactly how I feel. He loves me. For me. No conditions. And even though I wrestle with the idea of falling in love so quickly, there's something there. It's real. And he feels it too. I don't ever want to leave this bubble we're in, but I know our time is ending. I have to reenter the real world sooner or later. This can't last forever, although I desperately wish it could.

Our kisses are slow. Full of feeling. His gentle caress across my stomach matches his sensitive heart. The echo of his past marriage is touching, and it took everything in my power to hold back the tears. His love and devotion to her are something I've never experienced and thought only happened in movies. His vulnerability in sharing that piece of himself with me is something I will cherish deeply.

He stretches his arm, reaches under the tree, and hands me a box that looks hastily wrapped. This sudden shift catches me off guard.

"Will you open this now?" His amused tone makes me give him a questioning look.

"You want to do our gift exchange now?" I glance at the kitchen, doing mental calculations for cooking time. If we don't get the roast in the oven, we'll be eating this meal after midnight.

"No, not everything. But this one. I want you to open it before we get back in the kitchen." I look at the number of gifts under the tree, all in the same wrapping paper, and quirk an eyebrow at him.

"How did you get all this with our budget? Did you cheat?" There's no way he stayed within our hundred-dollar limit. My accusation hangs in the air.

"Nope. I'm not a cheater. Ever." The look he gives me resonates deep in my soul. He's not talking about our gift deal. He's honest. All the time. Rolling my eyes at his smirk, I get what he's implying.

"I went for quantity over quality. Here, open this." His eyes twinkle with mischief as I tear the paper to open the box. Anticipation outweighs my usual need to slowly and carefully unwrap a package. I think my days of prim and proper are long gone.

My full belly laugh breaks the silence and fills the room. Proudly, I hold the fabric against my chest and hug it tightly. It's incredibly thoughtful and absolutely perfect. A cartoon raccoon wearing a chef's hat adorns the apron, and it says, "My cooking is so awesome even the smoke alarms cheer me on."

"It's perfect!" I give him five quick kisses as a thank you. I hop up, buttoning my shirt, and throw the apron on over my head. This gift is the best because the guy who gave it to me really gets me.

"Come on, let's get this dinner started. I'm ready for my next cooking lesson."

We work in tandem, laughing and teasing as we destroy the kitchen. My tablet displays instructional videos that we constantly rewind, pause, and replay. Soon, the vegetables are chopped and seasoned. The meat is prepared. Honestly, it looks pretty good. So far. Once the meal is in the oven, I'm ready to collapse. Cooking is both exhilarating and exhausting.

One glance at the carnage in the kitchen, and my shoulders drop. The sink is overflowing with a jumble of dirty bowls, pans, and spoons. It may take me days to clean this kitchen. Strong hands massage my shoulders, and I immediately melt like butter on a hot stove. "Ohmygod, that feels amazing." I moan and lean into him, letting his fingers work my muscles.

"You're so tense. Why don't you go take a warm shower and let me clean up here?"

"But this is my mess."

"Our mess." He reaches into my hair and pulls something green from my messy ponytail. Parsley maybe? "Besides, you might feel better. Then we'll watch movies and open gifts before dinner. Sound good?"

Honestly, the way he puts my needs first is the best gift I could imagine. His kindness and consideration are something Trey never showed me. The more I'm around Sully, the more I realize how much I settled in my marriage. Sully's wife was a lucky woman.

Steam fills the bathroom as I take an extra-long, everything shower. My mind wanders as I daydream about the what-ifs and possibilities. What if I stay in North Carolina and start fresh? It's not the first time the thought has crossed my mind. But would Sully want me to stay? Do they need lawyers here? Maybe I could change careers and work in a store? Typically, these uncertainties would make me unbalanced and stressed. But today, I think nothing can take the Christmas joy from me. We promised to focus on the now. I'm considering amending our pact. I'm ready to think about the future.

TWENTY-ONE

SULLY

———

I can't keep myself from whistling while I wait for Cynthia to join me and for us to move on to the gift portion of the day. The sight of her face, lit up with delight at the apron, fills me with a proud, happy warmth. I worried my teasing might come off as criticism, and I definitely didn't want to undermine her self-esteem. Anticipation swirls in my belly as I consider her reaction to the other trinkets I bought her.

No doubt she assumed I wouldn't be able to pull off the cheap and absurd gift challenge, but little does she know that my kids only exchange silly gifts with me and their friends. We've been doing it since they were teenagers. What do you get the person who has everything and needs nothing? Things like custom-made socks with a portrait of their cat, apparently. I still send Ashleigh luxury items she wouldn't buy herself, but I know she cherishes the meaningful, fun gifts the most. I'm banking on Cynthia feeling the same way.

The arrangement of gifts is scattered on the table. The big one stays hidden, for now. I don't need her to think I broke our agreement. Technically, I didn't. I put the wheels in motion for this before we settled on the gift-giving rules. I hate using a loophole, but sometimes, that's what you have to do.

My phone vibrates on the counter, and I answer the family video call.

"Merry Christmas, Dad!" Julian and Alexander also say something but are drowned out by Ashleigh's happy sing-song greeting. Right on cue, the Decker men smile at her. She's the jewel of this family.

"Merry Christmas. Quick roll call, where is everyone?" My kids are living their best adult lives with partners I'm convinced Rebecca picked for them. Each found exactly who they needed and, most importantly, who loves them fiercely.

"Cole and I are in Charleston at his mom's house," Ashleigh says. I hear Cole say "Merry Christmas" in the background.

"Harper and I are in Raleigh with Chance and Lawson since they have a home game tomorrow," Julian says. Chance Fuller is Julian's best friend, and Lawson is Harper's brother. They play hockey for the Raleigh Renegades and are in the middle of their season.

"Dani and I have been up all night putting together Tyler's gifts. Why don't these things come assembled?" Alexander says in his usual gruff and grumpy tone. This is his first Christmas as a father, and he has a lot to learn.

"Yeah, I remember those days. And we never had enough batteries," I say with a chuckle.

"How are you, Dad? Are you sure you don't want to join us? You could fly out and be here in no time." As usual, Ashleigh worries about me. For once, it's unnecessary.

"I'm fine, really. You kids all have new families to start traditions with. I'm so damn proud of you all. We'll be together soon. I promise. I can't wait to meet my granddaughter." The shower just stopped, and while I'm not keeping Cynthia a secret, I'm not ready to share either. I can't imagine the grilling they'll give me.

"But, Dad," Ashleigh starts.

"I'll see you soon, sweetheart. Darcy has a little something for you for Christmas. I hope you like it."

"Darcy?" Cole peeks over her shoulder.

"She helped me with a little Christmas shopping. Look, I've got to go. Merry Christmas, Deckers."

"Ashleigh's a Davidson now." Cole kisses my daughter, his wife, on the cheek, an ear-to-ear grin filling his face.

"She'll always be my princess," I mumble. I'm still wrapping my head around the fact that my baby girl is a wife. "Love you."

"Love you too, but I don't think you were talking to me," Cynthia teases.

Startled, I disconnect and drop my phone on the counter. "Just my kids calling to wish me a Merry Christmas." As soon as the words leave my mouth, I instantly regret them. Kids. Holiday. Exactly what wounded her enough to hide in the mountains. But her smile never falters. There's no sign of her pretending like it's okay when it really isn't. She's finding her footing with her new life. New reality.

She sees the panic on my face and gives me a soft smile as she reaches for my hand. I'm caught off guard by her unexpected gesture, a gentle hand on my arm, as she tries to comfort me.

"It's okay. I sent a text to the kids, and at least they responded. My daughter isn't having the best time, but she's old enough to make her own decisions." She gives a little shrug.

"Well, you're right about that." I hope her kids will come to their senses and make a better decision when it comes to Cynthia.

"Yeah, lately I'm right about most things." She stretches to gently kiss me, but that isn't enough for me. I reach around and pick her up, carrying her to the couch, where I lay her down and cover her body with mine.

We make out like teenagers, tongues dancing while our hands roam. I'm insatiable with her. I consider having Dave live in my house when he returns so we don't break this spell. She's happy here. I'm not sure if it's me, the house, or the season, but I'm willing to freeze time to keep us like this.

"Hmmm, you're too good to be true. What do you see in an old man like me?"

She swats at my chest, playfully pushing me away. "What? You're old?!? Ewww." Her giggles surround me, and I can't resist the urge to tickle her to keep them coming. I may be old, but she makes me feel young. In between her laughter, she calls for me to stop, and I obey. I'll always follow her commands.

Tears from her laughter stream down her face, and I kiss them away.

"I'm sorry, did I go too far?"

"Oh, I don't know. Death by tickles and kisses sounds like a great way to go." She's still laughing as she puts her hand to her chest in an attempt to calm her racing heart.

"It's gift time!" Her hands come together in little claps, and I love watching her come to life before my eyes. I don't need gifts because she's the best present I could ask for. Thanks, Santa!

CHAPTER
TWENTY-TWO

CYNTHIA

———

Every haphazardly wrapped gift I open, with its lopsided bows and crumpled paper, contains something meaningful, funny, or both. I'm loving every second of this. I can't believe how much this man gets me in such a short time. He's picked up on my likes, dislikes, and quirks. And I've never said a word. He pays attention to the details.

After all those years of marriage, Trey still sent me red roses when he screwed up, which was often. I hate red roses. Always have. And now I equate them to another affair or forgotten special occasion. If I never see a red rose again, I'll be happy. But a bouquet of pink flowers? Love it. Every time. Do you think Trey ever sent me a pink bouquet? Nope. Never. And I told him over and over. I bought them for myself and had them in the house all the time. When his red roses arrived, they stuck out like a scarlet letter.

But Sully doesn't do that. Case in point: the last gift I open is a small LEGO set of pink flowers. I can guarantee Sully would never send me red roses.

"I love this! A do-it-yourself bouquet." I see the price tag and question his budget. Again.

"It was on sale. Scouts honor." His chuckle vibrates in his chest. "I know you enjoy puzzles, so I took a chance that you'd enjoy these flowers."

"I used to do them with the boys when they were younger. But why this set?"

"Well, you seemed to light up at the pastel flowers at the store, so I guessed."

And there you have it. Sully pays attention.

"Now your turn." I feel bad that my gifts aren't as thoughtful, but everything he opens, he tells me it's something he wanted but wouldn't have gotten for himself. When he opens the last box, he holds up the flannel shirt before rubbing it against his cheek. The blue plaid makes his eyes sparkle. I knew he'd look good in it. Blue is his color.

"It's perfect. I can't wait to see it on you in the morning." I don't miss the implication in his voice, and honestly, I'm looking forward to that too.

We settle in on the couch, snuggle under a blanket, enjoy a cup of his delicious hot chocolate, and watch some holiday romance movie. Given my current situation, this cheesy love story seems almost believable.

Sully's abandoned his favorite reading chair for me and the couch these days. His stack of books has shifted to the coffee table, his solitary life disrupted by me.

He gently plays with my hair; the soft touch is a distraction from the movie playing on the screen. His eyes, however, are on me.

"What?" His grin is hard to interpret.

"You're beautiful."

"Hardly."

"Definitely."

"I think you might need your eyes examined."

"Only to see you more clearly." He kisses me on my temple, and that gesture is more intimate than sex. It's caring. Possessive. Sincere. I snuggle in closer, Sully's comforting scent filling my senses, and close my eyes, savoring this precious moment.

The oven timer's alarm blares, a harsh sound that shakes me from a light sleep. My first thought was that I had triggered the smoke detectors again. Once my heart quits racing, I pull the roast from the oven, and a puff of steam hits me with the most scrumptious aroma. I carefully remove the cover and scoop the juices over the meat, then put it back in for the final fifteen minutes.

Without prompting, Sully sets the table. When he pulls out candles, I'm truly impressed. I can't imagine he had those sitting around for a formal occasion. He obviously bought them for our dinner. To make it special. I melt like butter on the vegetables.

"You did it. This is amazing. Even the most seasoned chefs have trouble with a standing rib roast, and you made it look easy."

"Hardly. But thank you for believing in me. Even when I don't. You've not only healed my torn and tattered heart, but my damaged self-esteem too." I wrap my arms around him and hold on for dear life. This wouldn't have been possible without this man's help.

We eat together, both making sounds normally reserved for the bedroom.

"Mmmmm, my god, this is better than any Michelin-star dinner." I'm all for praise, but that's a bit far-fetched.

"And how many Michelin restaurants are up here in the mountains?"

"None, but I think you should open one right away." Sully puts another forkful of food into his mouth and continues to make moaning noises.

"It's good, but let's not get carried away. I'm grateful it's not burned or raw or stuck to the bottom of the oven."

"Babe, I never doubt anything you put your mind to. If you want something, you'll get it."

With his unwavering belief in me, the foundation of my new life is being built brick by brick. I have the confidence to face the future. I'm prepared to start over. Stand on my own two feet.

I'm envious of Sully. His life is simple. He's not facing the pressures of the corporate world, although I sense he's worked the nine-to-five grind in the past. It's been a while since I've billed for my hours, and I'm worried I might have forgotten how. But just thinking about it lights an excitement I haven't felt in a very long time.

We finish dinner and put away the leftovers. Looking at the number of containers filling the refrigerator, I'm afraid we might be eating this for weeks. I search the internet for ideas to recycle them into new meals.

"You've become a real kitchen wizard, and I'm here for it." Sully kisses me on the temple, and that feeling of intimacy gives me butterflies. I swoon every time he does it. It's so caring. Possessive. It's one hundred percent Sully.

"I'm not sure about that, but I'll say you've made me enjoy cooking. My mother didn't think it was proper for a society wife to cook, and she never taught me. It's really fun. Especially with you."

"Everything is more fun with you. Even watching these sappy Christmas movies. Come on, I've got one ready for you." He takes his place on the couch and pats the spot next to him. I snuggle in, and it's exactly where I'm supposed to be.

I must have dozed off again because the fire is down to embers and the movie is over. Sully's awake, his fingers combing through my unruly waves.

"There's my sleeping beauty."

"What time is it?" I stretch my weary muscles.

"A little after midnight. So technically, it's not Christmas anymore. And now I can give you another gift." He's looking quite pleased with himself.

"Another gift? That's against the rules."

"I knew you were going to say that, but this isn't technically a Christmas gift. I got it before we made our pact. Are you ready?"

I screw up my mouth as I consider his working outside our deal. If I'm going to practice law again, I'm going to have to do a better job of shoring up the details. But he's got me here. On a technicality.

"You don't have to give me anything else. You've given me so much already."

"Well, this is something I've wanted to do since the day I met you." He steps out onto the deck, and the icy wind blows snow into the room. The chill wakes me up, and I pull the blanket around my neck. I didn't realize it was snowing, and when he turns the light on outside, I see the snowflakes dancing in the wind.

He closes the door and turns back, and I gasp when I see the gorgeously wrapped box. My mind reels with ideas of what this could be. He hands me the gift, and I'm instantly aware he didn't wrap this. And he didn't get it around here. The expensive paper is heavy, the creases sharp and straight. The silk ribbon forms a perfectly fluffy bow. A stark contrast to the earlier sloppily wrapped gifts. I can sense the excessiveness before I even open the box.

"Sully, I can't accept this. It's too much."

"You haven't even opened it yet." Disappointment fills his face, and I immediately feel bad for dashing his excitement.

"It's too nice to open. This wrapping is exquisite." The ribbon feels cool and smooth beneath my fingertips as I admire its subtle sheen. When I see the wrapping go under the lid, a sense of relief hits me. I don't think I could tear this gorgeous paper, even if it's meant to be disposable. "Well, you can guess I didn't do it. I had help with this because, well, it was out of my area of expertise."

I can't imagine who helped him. He's practically a hermit up here. I gently loosen the lid, slowly lifting it from the box, and stare at the signature orange box with the exclusive black ribbon. Oh no.

I shake my head and push it toward the table. "Sully, no. This is too expensive."

"You haven't even opened it yet." His voice sounds dejected.

"I hope this is a gag box. Because if it's real…"

"Just open it." His frustration is seeping through in his tone. I look at him, and he's annoyed. Not wanting to upset him, I open the box and let out a gasp. Nestled on the softest tissue paper is the most amazing vert jade Birkin I've ever seen. I don't know how he managed to buy a Birkin, but to get the color of your choice is unheard of. The certificate of authenticity shows it's new, purchased in Paris. It's not a resale.

"Sully, it's gorgeous." My hand passes over the soft leather and gently brushes the gold hardware.

"Sully…"

"Do you like it?"

"Of course. But I have so many questions. How? You don't just pick this up in town."

"Like I said, I had some help."

"Sully, this is so expensive. You can't spend your money on me like this." This bag is so much nicer than mine and costs tens of thousands of dollars. I'm confused and overwhelmed.

He sits next to me, and his hand cradles my face. "It's just money, and I have plenty. I've told you that. And I can spend it any way I want. As soon as I tried to clean up your bag, I started researching and, well, you probably know better than I do what's involved. I'm quite pleased with myself that I was able to pull it off. So please don't take this pleasure from me." His soft blue eyes plead with me, and I reluctantly relent.

"It's beautiful."

"So are you. The green matches your eyes. It was made for you, babe. Just say thank you and accept my gift. Please."

I swallow hard, take a deep breath, and do as he asks. "Thank you."

CHAPTER
TWENTY-THREE

SULLY

———

I breathe a sigh of relief as she accepts my gift. Given her fixation on money, I was extremely nervous she would balk at the price. Not that I blame her. Being insecure about paying bills isn't something I experience now, but I remember it when I was starting out. Money issues can eat at you. I do my best to pay my employees higher-than-average salaries to keep that feeling away. Being financially comfortable allows me to spoil my loved ones, and it brings me pleasure. It's for me as much as it is for her.

Her yawn is a reminder that it's well past our bedtime. I help her from the couch, and we make our way to bed. We're both tired, but I enjoy snuggling with her, inhaling her sweet fragrance, and holding her close just as much as I enjoy making love to her. At my age, intimacy comes in many forms, and I enjoy discovering all of them with Cynthia.

We've already fallen into a comfortable routine. I'm an early bird, waking up first and getting my work done while she sleeps in. Even though today should be a light workday, I can't reset my sleep cycle. When I wake at my usual six a.m., Cynthia's frantic packing puts me on high alert. Her sniffles are more than my heart can bear.

"Cynthia, what's going on? What's wrong?"

The sudden shock of being caught leaving catches her, and she freezes. Then, as if it's a natural reflex, she takes a deep breath, putting on that everything's-fine demeanor she had when we first met, and gives me a fake smile. I thought we were beyond that. I thought she could be honest with me. Disappointment and dread fill me as I wait for her response.

"I'm sorry I woke you." She turns from me and continues packing, no longer trying to be quiet about it.

After she puts a sweater in her suitcase, she zips it shut. The sound makes me shudder.

"Where are you going?" My morning voice, paired with my disappointment, sounds foreign—practically timid.

"Back to New York." She avoids eye contact. What did I do wrong?

"Why?"

"It's my home. My family is there." Her chin drops, and she says in a whisper, "They need me."

I'm out of bed now and step toward her. Confusion and disappointment swirl when anger joins my emotional party. "They need you? The same people who tossed you aside?" I know my barb hit when she bristles and steps back.

"Sully, don't. You don't understand. It's complicated."

"No, it's really not. It's toxic." She throws her shoulders back and refuses to back down. I'm proud of her for standing up for herself, but I wish it were about anything but this.

"How dare you! You don't know a thing about it."

I clench my jaw and temper my voice. "No. I don't. Because you wanted to leave our past out of any conversation. You weren't willing to trust me." My words hit the target once again. "So, tell me what's going on."

She won't meet my eyes. With her back to me, she recounts the events that led us to this moment, her voice barely a whisper. "Trey's wife and my daughter argued. I guess it got pretty ugly. Chloe reached out when she had a panic attack. I always help her through them, and I wasn't there for her." Pain fills her voice, the regret clear. "She needed me, and I wasn't there for her."

"Is she okay now?"

"Yes, but..." She shakes her head and turns from me. "You don't understand," she whispers.

"Oh, I understand." My frustration boils over, and I lash out, unfiltered words tumbling from me. "Your family has disrespected you for too long. They used your kindness and love to manipulate you into giving up your hopes, your dreams, your life for them. You mask your true feelings behind a facade of smiles, suppressing your desires because you've been made to feel unworthy. They treat you like the hired help, not a beloved mother. They do that because you allow them to do this to you." I'm seething but manage to keep my voice level. I'd never yell at her, but I'll also never lie to her. My truth is hard for her to hear, but not saying it is almost as damaging.

The sight of her tears, glistening on her cheeks, shatters my heart. It's the last thing I want to do. I never want to hurt her. I want to lift her up. Celebrate her. Live my life with her. But we can't think about the future without dealing with the past.

She grabs the handle of her suitcase and pulls it up. She works her bottom lip with her teeth, contemplating what to say. Her eyes meet mine, and I brace myself for her words, prepared for her to fight back. With the back of her hand, she wipes the tears from her face.

"I see. Well, I've got to go."

I put my hand on hers, hoping to stop her from leaving. My eyes beg her to stay. I want her to choose me.

"Sully." The sound of my name on her lips melts my resistance. I take her in my arms and kiss her, pouring out every ounce of love I have for her in that moment. I refuse to call this a goodbye kiss. But she needs to call the shots, not me. She needs to figure out what she wants. What she needs. I already know what I want. Her.

She pulls away, and her fake facade is back. "Sully, this has been wonderful and completely unexpected. You've shown me parts of myself I thought were lost. You've given me hope again. But my daughter needs me. I can't turn my back on her."

I understand more than she knows. If my daughter needed me, I'd drop everything, move heaven and earth to be there for her.

"Then go. Be with her. But promise me one thing."

"What's that?"

"When you figure out what you want for your future, just know I'd love to be a part of it. I'll always be there for you. Call me when you're ready."

"I will."

"I'll be waiting." With a nod of her head, she turns and leaves.

My head spins trying to put together what happened, but it doesn't matter. She's gone.

CHAPTER
TWENTY-FOUR

CYNTHIA

———

I'm back in New York because my daughter needed me. When I landed, I reached out, but my call went to voicemail, heightening my concern. A few hours later, she sent a text letting me know it all worked out. She's fine. I didn't need to come home. She didn't need me after all.

I'm angrier at myself than anyone else. Sully was right, but I had to come to that realization on my own. And I did.

I've been doing a lot of soul-searching these last few days. The life I've known is no more. But as each day passes, new dreams, new possibilities replace my melancholy. I'm making decisions that are best for me. I don't want my life to be a series of wash, rinse, repeat anymore. I want my future to be meaning-ful, purposeful. Exciting. Happy. Mine.

I'm attending my usual New Year's Eve gala—as a sort of farewell to the New York society life. It's time to ring in this year and welcome the new year with open arms. So here I am amidst the dazzling lights and formal attire, where everyone pretends that life is wonderful when it's not. I usually enjoy it. But not as much this year. Tonight, I crave the quiet solitude of a mountain cabin. I'd much prefer to be wearing an oversized flannel shirt, listening to a fire crackle, and watching the ball drop on TV. But I don't always get what I want. You think I'd be used to that by now. It's a good thing I've perfected my act of fake happiness. Because tonight, I'm wearing an all-too-snug emerald dress, smiling and chatting with people like this is exactly where I want to be. Another lie.

Grace and I step away from a group of people and make our way to the back of the room, where it's a little quieter. "Cyn, you practically rolled your eyes at Dan's story. Are you okay?" Grace hasn't left my side since I arrived. And now she's calling me out for not maintaining my typical fake social persona. I can tell she's watching me, but I'm fine. And I mean it this time.

"Yeah, I'm good. Has he always been that obnoxious?" Dan Humphrey is a pompous ass who stands on a moral high ground and judges others while behaving the same way. Maybe worse. He's the biggest gossip in New York social circles. I can only imagine what he's said about me over the years.

"Absolutely. I think we've just gotten used to him." She takes a sip of her champagne and looks around the room. "You still thinking about your flannel-wearing, blue-collared mountain man who called you killer?"

The glitz and glamour in the room are overwhelming. While I always thought my type was boardroom CEOs, I prefer a man who looks great in blue jeans and flannel.

"Yeah, he really made me stop and think about who I am and what I want. This isn't that appealing anymore."

"Did you decide about the job offer?"

Several weeks ago, I sent my resume to a recruiter to help me find a job. Yesterday, I received a call from a large law firm looking for a pro bono coordinator. When I interviewed today, it felt like the perfect fit. They offered me the job on the spot! I can even help with adoption cases.

The firm is based in New York but has offices in several cities, including one in Charlotte. Most of the work can be done remotely. If I accept, I just need to let them know where I want to be based.

"I'm taking the job. It's exactly the kind of work I want to do. I'm on the fence about staying in the city though." I look around the room at my so-called friends. Except Grace, obviously. She's the real deal. Getting a fresh start could be what I need. And while Charlotte isn't in the mountains, it's at least in the same state.

"I'd miss you terribly, but if you're asking me, I think you should go be with your mountain man." She wraps her arm around my waist and puts her head on my shoulder. "I'll come stay at Dev's place, and we'll be neighbors."

We both laugh. I'm not sure if it's from the champagne or the impending goodbye.

Then, the strangest thing happens. The kind of thing that only happens in movies, but never in real life. But it's happening. In MY real life. The crowd parts, and I see Sully talking to Devlin Millbanks.

What's he doing here? Maybe Devlin invites his employees to this party, and I never noticed?

"Who's caught your eye?" Grace follows my line of sight and focuses on Sully. "Sullivan Decker?"

"What's he doing here?" I'm surprised, but in a good way.

"He's Devlin's best friend. Swoony, isn't he? I've always had the biggest crush on Sully, but he was totally devoted to his wife, which made him even more attractive if you ask me. She died years ago, and I don't think he's dated since. Probably not the easiest thing to do when you're a billionaire."

"He's a billionaire? Like with a B?!?" I barely get the words out when I begin to connect the dots. My self-loathing strikes again. Me and my stupid pact. I shake my head in disbelief.

It all starts flooding back, each piece clicking into place. Sully never said he was the caretaker. I just assumed. He told me several times that money wasn't an issue. Like with the Birkin. And he said he hadn't been up on the mountain long. I thought he meant he wasn't from there, not that he'd just gotten there. I can't believe I didn't know. I feel like an idiot.

He glances in our direction, and suddenly, our eyes meet, and a spark ignites. The room brightens as his face fills with a familiar grin.

Turning toward me to continue with her gossip, Grace is totally unaware he's walking this way. "Yeah, he and Devlin made their money in the early days of the tech boom. Now he lives in Charlotte and owns the Carolina Reapers. And the incredible mountain house next to Devlin's, of course. They're total opposites and baseball rivals, but their friendship trumps it all. Do you want me to introduce you?"

"That's not necessary, Grace," he says in his baritone voice. "You look incredible, killer."

Grace's eyes grow as wide as saucers. Her boisterous laughter causes people to look our way, and I drop my eyes to the floor. OH. MY. GOD. Hot flash or embarrassment or need— or maybe all three—hit me all at once, and I'm burning up from head to toe. I probably resemble a confused traffic signal, what with my green dress and flushed face.

"SULLY is your flannel-wearing orgasm king?!" She squeals with excitement, clapping her hands and bouncing on her toes. I don't remember the last time I saw her this excited.

"Orgasm king, is it?" he says with a chuckle. His fingertips are under my chin, and he gently raises my head so my eyes meet his. Though I'm completely mortified, his touch alone triggers a flashback to the cabin, and the heat washes over me again.

The midnight blue of his tuxedo accentuates the bright, lively sparkle of his eyes. Blue is most definitely his color. And I knew he'd look fantastic in a suit, even though I still prefer him in flannel.

Gathering the courage to look at him, I'm met with a humorous expression, his whole smile crinkling his eyes.

"I may have shared a little about our time together." I nervously shift back and forth on my feet, and my face feels like it's on fire. I wish the ground would swallow me whole.

With a little chuckle, he asks, "Just not my name?" He's enjoying the teasing a little too much. But I don't care. I'm thrilled to see him.

"I guess not." I shrug. I'm trying to be nonchalant, but it's near impossible. "Did you know I thought you were the handyman?"

"Yeah, I tried to tell you, but you made the rules. Honestly, I'm not much of a handyman."

"Oh, I don't know. You're pretty handy to me."

"I mean, I can't really fix things."

"You can fix the most important things." Curiosity fills his face. "You fixed my broken heart."

"Well, in that case, I'm a damn good handyman, I guess."

Grace has been watching us go back and forth, her head moving like she's watching a tennis match. She steps between us, grabs my shoulders, and shakes me. "I can't wait to tell Devlin. You guys, I don't know. Kiss! Reunite! Live happily ever after! Ekk! I'm so excited!" She releases me and scurries off into the crowd, leaving us alone. I'm nervous. I'm not sure where we go from here.

"Everything okay with your daughter?" His sincere concern is apparent in his expression. His question is a stark reminder of why we aren't cuddling on a couch in a remote mountain cabin right now.

"It turns out she didn't need me after all." I cock my head to the side and shrug. I wait for the dejection and despair I've been carrying around these past few days, but it doesn't appear. I'm relieved neither does his *I told you so.*

"You didn't call." I don't miss the disappointment in his voice.

"Yeah, I know. I've been busy." That's true. But I also wasn't sure what to say. I should never have left him. But I needed to learn my lesson. And I did. The hard way.

Realizing it sounds like I'm blowing him off, I rush to explain. "I got a job offer today, and the first person I wanted to call was you." I can tell by his expression that he wants to know why I didn't.

"But I was embarrassed to admit you were right." Admitting that my family has moved on is a hard pill to swallow. But somehow, having Sully here, it's going down a little easier.

"That's one thing I wish I weren't right about. I'm sorry." He reaches down and takes my hand, giving it a gentle squeeze. He makes everything better.

"Me too, but I'll be okay." And I will.

"So, you got a job?" Typical Sully. He has an uncanny ability to notice every detail, never missing a thing.

"I did. I'll be heading up a pro bono division for a firm based in the city." My excitement for the job boosts my confidence and washes away my embarrassment.

"That's wonderful. It's exactly what you wanted. I'm so proud of you." He's still cautious. Hesitant. Leaving him without a backward glance still weighs heavily on my heart. Yeah, I made a big mistake. I hope he's as forgiving as he is loving.

"Thanks." I know now's the time to leap. Go for what I want.

"The catch is," I say, shuffling my feet. "I'll be moving to Charlotte. I'll need to find a place to live, but I think a new city is what I need for a fresh start." I wince, anxiously awaiting his response.

"Well, I might know a place if you're interested." A playful glint shines in his mischievous eyes. He gives me one of his flirty winks, and I know I've made the right decision. He's my new family. My chosen family.

I reach up and wrap my arms around his neck, pulling his face down to mine, and give him a kiss not suited for public viewing. But what do I care? I won't be seeing these people again.

Someone clears their throat, and we break apart like teenagers caught making out by our parents. I can feel the heat rise up my neck and face again. Sully's forehead rests against mine as we catch our breath, and I can't contain my giggles. I'm practically giddy about how this year is ending. And the start of next year is looking promising too.

"Dad, I thought you weren't supposed to kiss until midnight?" The handsome young man and his date look at us curiously. His bright-blue eyes light up with amusement.

"Hi, I'm Julian Decker, and this is my girlfriend, Harper Cartwright. I'm VERY pleased to meet you." His familiar grin looks just like Sully's. Julian pulls Harper close and kisses her on the temple as she melts into his side. I bet I know where he learned that move.

Well, I guess I might see SOME of these people again after all. And that's just fine with me.

ALSO BY CHERYL CAMPBELL

Trouble at First: Ashleigh and Cole

The Decker Connection series starts with Ashleigh and Cole 🥎

All Ashleigh Decker wants this summer is to be the social media intern for the Savannah Pajamas. Is that too much to ask? She's off to a great start until she meets a player who is nothing but trouble.

This summer league is the perfect opportunity for Cole Davidson to impress the MLB scouts. His dream to play first base for the Carolina Reapers is within his grasp. An added bonus? A beautiful intern who steals his heart.

The only problem? She's hiding her identity. Her father is the owner of the Reapers, and her overprotective older brother is the General Manager. Can Ashleigh keep her secret and the guy without jeopardizing his career?

Sliding into Home: Matt and Darcy

Overwhelmed doesn't begin to describe my life. I'm in over my head remodeling a multi-million-dollar beach house. It's the only thing standing between me and college graduation. Then the guy I've crushed on since middle school offers to be my assistant. Did I mention he's my brother's best friend? Yep. Matt Hartman, swoony boy next door and professional baseball player, is working side by side with me this fall. It takes everything I have to keep my feelings for him contained, until, well, I don't. Can I put his friendship with my brother on the line for a relationship with me?

I've hit more milestones this year than most do in a decade. I graduated from college, got drafted into Major League Baseball, played on a triple-A team in my hometown, and now, for the first time in my life, I'm enjoying my off-season. But am I? When I'm presented with the opportunity to help Darcy Davidson with her senior project, I gladly volunteer my services. It's something to fill my time, and besides, my best friend's sister needs help. That's all it is, right? Then why do I want to be so much more than her assistant?

Living the Suite Life: Alexander and Dani

Stress and pressure come with the territory when you're the youngest General Manager in the MLB. Add in my self-appointed role as the protector of the Decker Connection, my tight-knit group of siblings and friends, and it's no wonder they say I'm grumpy.

I'm facing down a public relations nightmare after one of my players assaults someone at a local food festival, and this PR problem is about to push me over the edge. Then I meet this full-of-sunshine, rainbows from storm clouds, heart-full-of-kindness, single mother, and I'm in more trouble than I ever imagined. There's absolutely no saving me from falling now.

The Final Draft: Julian and Harper

Julian Decker's billion-dollar sports agency represents the top athletes in the world. His charm, success and sexy blue eyes have landed him on the hottest bachelor list for the past five years. He's a hopeless romantic, with money, fame, and a rotation of beautiful women on his arm each week. Some would say he has it all. But things aren't always as they seem. Behind the flashing lights and camera clicks, Julian has deep-seated trust issues and a secret he keeps hidden, even from his closest friends in the Decker Connection.

Harper Cartwright is tired of being known as "the hockey player's sister" and is ready to forge her own path. With her master's degree in hand, she's headed to New York to learn from the best and make her author dreams come true. It's a whole new ball game for her. A new city. A NHL goalie roommate and his adorable dog. An intense and demanding writing program. She has a lot on her plate. Harper's handling all these life challenges until she encounters Julian Decker, a handsome playboy with a panty-dropping smile. His intense pursuit of her has Harper excited and wary, especially after she discovers his secret.

LET'S CONNECT

Cheryl loves connecting with readers and talking about the Deckers. Join her in the conversation. Follow for sneak peeks and behind the scenes fun.

And don't forget to leave a review on Amazon 😃

Cheryl Campbell Facebook Cheryl Campbell Author

Cheryl Campbell Instagram @Cheryl_Campbell_Author

Cheryl Campbell TikTok @cherylcampbellbooks

To purchase signed copies, visit her website at cherylcampbellauthor.com

Want to hear the Decker Halls playlist? Check it out on Spotify.

Decker Halls Playlist on Spotify